Get over it

by

F. Linday

Onwards and Upwards Publications
Berkeley House
11 Nightingale Crescent
West Horsley
Surrey
KT24 6PD
England

Adventures by

www.onwardsandupwards.org

ISBN: 978-0-9561037-7-2

Cover design: Leah-Maarit Jeffery
Printed and bound in Great Britain by
CPI Antony Rowe, Chippenham and Eastbourne

Acknowledgements

Huge thanks go to my husband, Will and our grown up children Amy, Ben and Hannah. I couldn't have done it without their love and support.

Thanks to my fab sister Liz and husband John for believing in me along with a few others. You know who you are.

Also, due to the generosity of Arts Training Central, I've benefited from the experience and skills of a marvellous mentor, called Gwen Grant.

Finally, I have to thank the Association of Christian Writers for their encouragement leading me to Onwards and Upwards Publishers, Mark and Diana.

Contents

1. ABOUT ME, RUNNING AWAY

I first met Athena when we dropped anchor in the bay. She was about my age and gorgeous, with all this long black hair. She was just smiling at me from outside her dad's café. But it was her incredible smile that reminded me of my far-off Mum. So I made sure I bumped into Athena not long after we got there and that's when she told me where her name came from. Only this Greek goddess diva! "I'm named after the Madonna statue, the one that looks over us all from the hilltop," she'd said.

"Wow!" came my lame response. Her big eyes got me. But the goose bumps she gave me were good. I could cope with them. They masked the empty feeling and let me blank out the only woman who'd ever meant anything to me.

I had to face it that for this holiday, it was only my dad and me 'doing' the Greek islands. Not conventionally but the cool way. It was over two weeks ago, I got a taxi from the airport and it dropped me off at the harbour. And there in front of me was this awesome boat.

I knew what kind of boat it was because my dad had e-mailed me and that made me Google it. It was a sleek, forty-foot, grey catamaran, sleek being my dad's word. The first time I saw it, sparkling on the water, the harbour was a clear blue and looking around the jetty at the other boats, I could see this catamaran was the best one there. It looked like a Lego special! Double hulls, according to him, and it had these neat kinda folded sails, as well. Pretty special, I thought, especially packed with a couple of Yamaha engines giving us forty-horse power.

Once I got on it, I couldn't stop Dad giving me this full demo of the windshield extending to make a cockpit tent. He goes, 'You do this, do that,' and out of nowhere comes some sort of clear plastic frames that make a roof. Not a bad toy, I suppose. Basically, it stops you from getting wet. He went on about life jackets and safety drills and stuff and stuff and more stuff. Like it's going to catch fire on all that water. As if! So I felt safe, well, safe...ish! Considering.

Earlier that month, back home, I wasn't completely fazed when it dawned on me Mum couldn't make it. I should have known. But lately, the real and unreal are whirling around in my head, doing their own thing. Anyway, since then I agreed to come along to help my dad out. But I didn't want to come. I was doing him a favour, although why I should I really don't know.

After all, he's never done anything for me.

That whole Navy thing he did for his precious country, not me. Then he keeps saying, "It's a good life in the Navy." Well, it might have been for him but it wasn't for me. And where did Mum come in this? I hardly know him really, because he's not been around ever since I can remember.

Anyway, Mum's just not here so he's 'It'.

We'd come out to Greece because he couldn't stand the house, not like it was with all those soppy cards around. Yuck! Time they went but I couldn't tell him. In those first few weeks after our lives were ruined, he'd stood there, my dad, trying to make tea. Frozen pizza. Burnt yet again! Rubbish!

Every time he went in the kitchen the fire alarm would go off, so I would wander through, "Am I off to the chippy then?" I would ask, rubbing it in.

That's when he says, "No, but how do you fancy a donner kebab?" Showing off for a change, I thought, but this time I see in his face that he actually means what he's saying. "I've thought about this," he goes on, "and we could do it. We could disappear. Go somewhere warm, Greece say?"

I tried to figure him out.

"Do what? You're not serious, are you?"

"Deadly," he said, before he could stop himself.

I almost choked and Dad went bright red but neither of us said anything. Anyway, I agreed to give it a shot, us hanging out on this trip but I knew me and Dad had a long way to go before we felt real together.

My great escape started badly when I'd hated being this sad loser on the endless flight from London to Rhodes with some dumb, fussy flight attendant thinking she owned me. One actually touched my hair! What was that all about? In my head I screamed, 'I'm not having that!' And, 'I'm not doing the stupid label thing they want to hang around my neck, either.' It was all my dad's fault. I couldn't believe that he'd actually paid extra to have me watched. So I'd put my earphones back in and hid their stupid 'sky flyer solo' tag.

If he couldn't trust me travelling alone, why did he even bother? Especially, treating me like some dumb kid.

All because once, just once, I did a runner. It was the 21st of July. Well, I had good reason to. I was stressed. And he knows it. Okay, he got worried but since then he thinks I need an A.S.B.O. or something, to keep me in check.

Surprisingly, I have to say he started well. My dad on his great escape! This loner stuff suited him. He was entirely on top of everything, having hired the boat the week before and already sailed across from the mainland, no problem. That's the week I got to crash at my mate Ben's. Straight after, it all kicked off. I was doing traumatic loss apparently! No wonder that even though I kept my body moving on my skateboard I just crashed and burned, I couldn't do it. My head just wasn't right! I knew I had to stick with my dad. And after travelling all that way my dad goes and greets me with horns blaring. An extreme cringe factor!

I nearly headed back home right then.

Rubbing his hands, he couldn't wait for me to get on the boat and started shouting, "Johnny, my man, jump on. How was your flight, son?"

As if the horn wasn't bad enough. Johnny, my man! Who is that guy? Not me. Not for the past ten years, anyway.

"It was boring," I let him know.

He took a step backwards.

"Oh! Shame," he went, then revved up again. "Well, that's no good. We don't want you bored, do we? We'll have to sort that one out, won't we mate?"

This man was a fool. He was aggravating me already. And I wasn't his mate, either.

The boat was kind of neat though, so I went along with him, asking, "What's its top speed?"

My dad beamed.

"Now you're talking. Twelve knots. It'll do twelve knots and leave all the others standing." What he didn't say was that it could only thrash the rest if he accidentally forgot the hire agreement rules. I found this out when I was kidding him about where the turbo boost was. He hated me being sarcastic but what did I care? He talked as if this dumb boat was his baby or something.

So, all I said was, "Really."

By his reaction, I saw I was meant to be more impressed.

"Yeah, well," he said. Then, "Hungry?"

"Why? What's up for burning this time?" I asked.

Dad tried to laugh but I wasn't being funny and I don't think he found it funny. Not really.

"You wait and see, young man," he said, reaching out to clip me one. As if he would ever be quick enough. When he missed he shrugged and went on, "Well, there are all sorts of meals packed in the galley. Luckily, most of them don't need much cooking. It's easy, you just shove them in the microwave, so help yourself."

What's he like? I'm sick of shoving things in the microwave but all I said was, "Okay, I'll grab something in a bit."

Dad took my holdall and dumped it on the deck. "We'll see

to that later," he said, then got me helping him winding in ropes to free us from the moorings.

"Do this. Do that," he goes.

But bossing people about comes naturally to him. That's all he's done for twenty years. Before we'd finished there was a small crowd watching us go out of the harbour. I looked at them and thought, yeah, right, you wish. Dream on. It was the first time I'd felt good in ages.

So, giant sails flapping, we sailed out of Rhodes Town harbour, Dad flying this huge Union Jack. What a poser! I suppose it was just in case someone had missed the sound of that horn.

'Tom Cat' was the name of the catamaran and it was a real mean machine. Tucking my head in, I squeezed down the few steps to the cockpit at the back where Dad slept. He'd shown me a cramped bit in the middle for me on the same side.

"You can have the double if you like, plenty of room," he'd said, pointing ahead.

This double bunk fascinated me. It was a whole lot bigger than where Dad had first put me but the idea of sleeping in that long front hull freaked me out.

Too claustrophobic, for sure!

Plus, Dad was just next door and I needed to keep an eye on him.

2. ATHENA ON MY MIND

If she'd come with us she could have put her stuff in my cabin. I would have shoved up for her. No trouble.

As we sailed over the next few days, I found out the boat wasn't bad the way it was fitted out. You could get loads of gear in but thanks to me the place soon looked a pit. Hey, what was there to tidy up for? It wasn't big enough really, although Dad said it was the biggest he could hire. More excuses. He was good at them.

What I liked best was just lying in the sun on deck, chilling out, watching him rush around. I noticed he was getting stressed out when it went windy because he shouted something about ducking my head.

"BOOM!" he roared, then, "Johnny, will you get your head down?"

"Yeah, yeah, give me a break, will ya?" I said, making out I'd seen this enormous trunk of wood wafting my way. I wouldn't have come if I'd known about this. Couldn't he see I was busy reading a text joke from Paul? It was that bad it was good!

Then I watched him get on with all the technical stuff when the boat wasn't leaning too much but still he had a go at me. Above the sound of my iPod I heard, "Johnny!" followed by, "Shift onto the nets if you want to survive this trip!"

So I hutched along and eyed up the dinghy for my chances of ever getting some peace. At least if I was in that I would have my own space. Do my own thing.

The day before, when the sea was crashing and bashing about, and it does do that, I had to go back to bed because I didn't get the point. I mean, Dad had two perfectly good engines but he hardly ever used them! Surely we could outrun the waves? But instead all he said was, "Let's go and catch some wind," getting far too excited and wasting precious energy.

I just ended up feeling bad in my stomach.

I went along with him though. "Way to go," I would say, leaving Dad to mess with his satellite navigation gadget and get us out of some squally weather.

"What you've got to understand about the sea, Johnny," he says, "is the way it can change from flat calm to waves over six metres high! And it does that," he wags his finger at me like a teacher, "all within a blink of an eye."

Then he started trying to bore me with knot-tying lessons as if it was a matter of life or death but I dodged him, locking myself in the micro loo to text my mate Ben. Much more relevant. Trouble was, not much to tell him.

I came up on deck in the afternoon, rating the awesome never-ending summer blue sky. It was just like the Cornish sky where me and Mum used to go the first week of the summer hols. From way back. We went almost every year. Well nice! But in Greece the wind blows strongest in the late afternoon and that is when the flat horizon goes wobbly, not in a good way, either.

When he eventually got that I couldn't handle rough weather

on the boat as it made me puke, me and my dad walked along the beach. We were laughing our heads off at the weird accents we heard around us. Mostly though, we didn't speak. That night it was calm again and the sun just melted into the sea. Something else! That's when I got the fishing tackle out. Nothing fancy, just a cheap weight and hook on a plastic line wrapped around some cork. For bait we used out-of-date sandwiches begged off the Dionysos café. Athena and her family were all right looking after us like that. She showed me the best spot, off the pier and the stale bread did the trick and I caught plenty. Athena was my living, laughing prompt to keep going.

Apparently, Dad told me, the mornings were good for fishing, too, but I passed on them. I soon learnt my lesson because the one time I did stagger on deck early, flashing his Navy tattoo, he tried some weird man-hug kind of thing on me.

Then, all awkward, he said, "I'll show you just how it's done, son." Seeing I was not convinced he went on, "Cos the sea is my backyard." Bizarre! Yeah, right, I thought, what exactly could Dad show me? He'll give his orders and the fish'll jump out standing to attention. I don't think!

He was new to this 'chilling' game because he'd spent most of his life at work and now Mum had dropped him right into uncharted territory, even for him.

So when Dad started fishing I watched the so-called master at work. Not exactly riveting! He just caught a couple of puny black and white stripy fish.

But I told him, "Not bad for an old man, considering," reminding him he only had twenty minutes to go before it started getting dark.

"Don't push it," he grunted back. "I know what you're up to, trying to put me off. It won't work. Now, just let me do this." He hardly budged and I could tell he badly wanted to beat my score. Trouble is, I'd got four decent sized eaters in an hour. I was the champion! Still, he thought he had a chance. Well somebody had to. He was quite brown, okay, but he was losing his hair faster than he'd like to admit which explained the cap glued to his head 24/7.

Poor old man!

"Bring them on, Dad," I jeered, "go on, do your worst."

Dangling my wide feet over the pier, it made me smile noticing these huge shoals of fish giving his bait a wide berth. All the same, I half wished I could look like my dad, a golden brown basted turkey thingy because his weathered look might suit me. I didn't stand a chance though, for with him having been in the Persian Gulf for months, he'd got a serious head start on his tan. Whereas, I knew I just looked a bit scary with my dangling bleached dreadlocks. The castaway look did me no favours with my red and blotchy skin.

Anyway, nothing much was happening, so I thought I'd have another go at winding him up.

"What are we doing for tea tonight? Cos I'm starving."

No response, only a sigh. I would have to try harder.

"Well, I'll just have to eat the rest of your bait then," I said, "and declare myself the outright winner," knowing this would do it.

He went mad.

"Don't you dare touch that bait," he roared. "I've got a whole ten minutes to catch a whopper yet and those sandwiches are so old they'll give you the belly ache, anyway."

He had a point.

But then he spoilt it going on about, 'all this fresh air and snorkeling is doing your appetite so much good,' stuff and looking real smug, but I knew he was trying hard to stop me getting to him.

"Don't kid yourself," I said, "it's just cos there's no tele!" That shut him up. Then I went on, "Have you done yet?" and when he didn't answer, I stood up. "It's getting a bit cold. I'm off to see Athena and check out what the dish of the day is at the café."

As I padded along the wooden boards I could hear him chuntering behind me, declaring a draw due to his reduced time. 'Now you're both even,' I could hear my mum say, in my head. Like she did, always smoothing things over. I didn't want to share that with him.

"I'll get you tomorrow, though, don't think I'll let you off cos it's your birthday," Dad interrupted my thoughts. He could never accept defeat like a man.

What a cheat! Who cares? Whatever! I wasn't going to waste any more breath. He'd apparently remembered my birthday though, amazing. I'd forgotten all it about it. Tomorrow must be the 27th October, came to me.

The café Dionysos was just a short walk along the sands and

I knew they would make us feel welcome. I had our entire catch splashing about in my special little kiddy sandcastle bucket, so I made sure no one could see me even though it was nearly dark. When I found a skinny cat outside the café, I dumped the bucket and let her dip her paw in. One by one she helped herself. Crunchy!

By now Dad had caught up, so I pointed to the cat.

"You'll have to catch bigger ones tomorrow, Dad. This kitten would still be hungry after your measly small fries. All I can say is, it's a good job he had my whoppers to fill his belly!"

"Ha. Ha. Very funny," he snorted, then, marching into the café he looked around. "Now where're we sitting?" He had to be kidding.

He was too late, anyway, because I'd already pulled my chair up to the bar where Athena was serving.

We had a quick chat, "What you up to, Athena?" I asked.

"Nothing. Only work."

"Shame!"

Then she went on, "What about you?"

"Me?" I said. "I've just been messing about mostly. My dad's doing my head in, you know what I mean?" I loved her smile. "What's the special tonight?" I asked, before she had to go and take someone's money. "I'd better let my dad know or he'll come over and bug me." I didn't want my dad to tell her about my birthday, either. Spooky though, her dad's being the day before mine.

Athena grinned, "You're in luck. It's a naming day. Today it's my dad's turn to celebrate so it's our house speciality. Lamb souvlaki."

I took my dad the cold beer Athena had poured for him, passing on the message about the lamb skewer thing.

"Here you go," I said, putting the iced glass into his hand. "Shall I order that for you since you're all right sitting with your pals?"

He looked at me then at the people on the table next to him who he'd been chatting to. I knew they were talking about the weather back home. That's all Brits ever seem to talk about.

"Right," he said, "okay," and reaching in his pocket, he pulled out some Euros to keep me quiet. "Yeah, okay, that sounds fine," he went on.

My dad had his uses.

Back at the bar, I gulped a pint of ice-cold coke down until it gave me brain freeze. Thinking of what I wanted to eat after all those snacks and fishy bits on the boat, I ordered some proper food. Steak and chips with all the trimmings.

Watching Athena and her family, I wanted them for my family. They were so together. Anyway, because it was Demetrius Day, Athena's dad was well happy. All he had to do was enjoy himself. They poured Ouzo onto the tiled floor and lit it!!! Ace. And then her dad started this weird dance move. I've never seen anything like it. He looked a bit like our star Melton goalie, Tommo, arms outstretched with the ball going nowhere. But instead of the football, it was glasses being thrown onto the floor. And I mean, on purpose. As well, he had his knees proper bent, looking painful. He did the odd high kick when some men, probably more Demetriuses, linked arms. I grabbed my mobile to take a snap and sent it to Ben with a message, 'Grees rox!'

But that wasn't the best thing that happened. The best thing was when Athena took hold of my arm and we stood there together. She made me feel like I mattered. It was as if, somehow, there was just the two of us in an empty café, the loud music gone so that all I heard was her laughter and all I saw was her face. I wanted that moment to last forever.

Nothing exciting ever happened like that back home. And it was never going to, either.

I wanted to say, "Athena, what just happened?" But I was scared to mess up because what if nothing had happened for her? I wondered if she'd even noticed my arm around her waist. Anyway, it was too late to ask because the moment was gone and the café was bustling again. Then again, I can't have frightened her off too much because Athena didn't move and she easily could have done.

"They're mad here on naming days," she said. "Hang around here long enough and you'll soon find out that's what they are. Crazy people! You need to listen to me." She did that thing with her eyelashes, like a fluttering thing, just for me. Or so it seemed. Then she was gone to serve another table but I still felt all tingly where her hand had leant on mine.

It was quite warm in the café. After a while, Dad joined me at the bar and I felt myself nodding but I tried to keep my eyes open to follow Athena around the room. I managed to half listen to my dad. We happily left the bar when it came to clearing up time, both of us being crap at that.

I said, "See you later," to Athena. She gave me a wave goodbye. Dad being clever said, "Adio" and we at last agreed on one thing, that it had been a really good night. Then we dawdled our way along the beach catching the cool reflections on the lid of the sea.

Back on deck after a shaky dinghy ride, where he actually let me row, he banged on a bit. And of course, we had to have the war- his favourite subject. He was showing off some more about keeping the peace, mostly by blowing people's heads off! How does that work? Like that made any sense.

Then he said, "It's important we remember what's happened in these conflict situations so we don't make the same mistakes again."

Who was this we? I hated his royal 'we'. All it did was make me realise how much I missed home and my best mate, Ben, who didn't need to show off. So I got my phone to text him for some seriously sane talk.

'Ben, mate! Wot u up 2? Dad's doin me hed in. Tb b4 I lose it!!!' When he heard my message send tone, Dad started up again.

"John, are you listening? Who are you texting at this time of night?"

"Ben, that's all. Okay? It was just Ben if you really must know." I shrugged my shoulders.

Then he began digging a bigger hole saying, "Johnny, now listen. This is it. Life isn't a rehearsal."

Glancing at the dinghy again, I yawned, "I know, I know." Feeling a lecture coming on, I tried to avoid it. "Anyway, I've had it. I'm off to bed," disappearing down into the cockpit sharp-ish before he got too heavy.

Dad had wound me up with what he'd just said. Life isn't a rehearsal. Yeah, give me a break. I knew that last year, thanks very much. On my own. There I was on a wicked father and son weekend with church, having a great time go-carting, fishing, hiking and camping, but the only thing was I went with Paul, the youth leader. Ben's dad managed to be there for him. But not my dad. No. He couldn't even be in the same country. So what right had he to start lecturing me?

I heard the so-called Captain shouting, "Night," while I read my text back from Ben. Ben sounded really busy with the girls, 'Cum bk Jon, need ya ere.'

Tempting.

I flopped onto my bunk and shut my eyes. Athena was there again. I liked that bit but my head was full of other rotten stuff that wouldn't shift. Wounded, I asked God, "why me?" Result! Der! God must be on his hols, too. That's why I'd been dropped right in all this.

That helped me fall off to sleep.

Then, in my dream, my mum gave me a nice new hoodie.

3. WHEN DAD COULDN'T HANDLE IT

I didn't know how long I'd slept but when I woke the cabin was still dark. I got that my dad hadn't come to bed because his sleeping bag wasn't messed up. It was probably the noise from another drunken Demetrius that had woken me and prompted me to look out of the porthole. I couldn't see much. Just stars, a blurred view of the beach and café beyond. Then a staggering man came into shot. This shadowy figure was falling about making some terrible noises like a pig grunting and squealing. Funny. At first.

That's when I heard my dad shouting, "Go steady, old man," then, "what's your game?"

Forget trying to sleep. No such luck! For the drunk his party continued. Yeah right, he was loud but he didn't need Dad bellowing at him. I glanced at my mobile and saw 1 new message. That'd be Ben, making it about 2 o'clock here and mid-night back home, the limit of his curfew. Two, stupid o'clock!

Then, "Go home to your bed!" I heard Dad holler over the blankness of the sea.

I couldn't stand the pressure, so I pulled my shorts on and clambered up the steps on deck, squinting as the mast light stung my eyes. My dad was hopping mad by this time.

"What's up?" I asked.

"Just look," he cried, "The fool's trying the 'light the floor trick' with the leftover Ouzo. Twice, there have been huge flames shooting from that bottle. I was just nodding off here on deck when the glare woke me."

"Chill-out Dad," I said. "It's not your problem." Then I regretted it instantly. Bit harsh, that. "He's not doing any harm." I was still half asleep, well that's my excuse. Dad was folding up a map of the islands but still he didn't take his eyes off the beach. I refused to believe he was getting itchy feet again and that he was even thinking of sailing on. Not now we were enjoying it all so much and starting to settle.

"What I'm worried about," Dad began, "is the daft old fella setting fire to the tablecloths or those wicker partitions. A fire in that café would cause as much damage as a storm at sea and…" He went on, I cut off.

Typical!

Dad couldn't be happy just looking after us; he had to poke his nose in the Greeks' business, too. I wish he bothered that much about me. "Sod it all!" Falling into a chair I shut him out. And that was when my Uncle Paul's voice came into my head. We'd been digging about in maps, as well. Me and him. Not like Dad, on his own.

'You'll have to let me know where you are,' Paul had said, 'then I'll be able to track your journey.' This was when I crashed at Ben's house. Then he'd gone on, 'you know, a few thousand years ago, the apostle Paul travelled by boat to Greece.' Now I imagined our Paul marking us on his map. In dock at Kindos Bay, what I called Athena's Bay.

That time, we'd found some bizarre place names and I'd joked, 'I just hope my dad's maps are better than these or we'll be heading for BIG trouble,' but Paul had said he wouldn't be leaving our safety to luck, not with the Mediterranean Sea being so dangerous.

'I'll be praying for you the entire trip,' he'd said, finishing with, 'you're a solid lad, John and you've come so far lately and I've complete faith in you.'

This faith thingy, believing in what you can't see, buzzed around my head whilst my full attention jumped to what I could see, going on near the beach. Wow! Like, after this huge flash there was a bright orange glow, a great 'Whoosh!' sound and an echo from the beach of, "Arrrrr!"…Followed by silence. Mental.

Help! Dad had been right. The drunken fool was setting the cafe on fire. My dad jumped to his feet because there on the shore our Taverna burst into flames. I just froze. But my dad went into fire fighter mode, untying the dinghy rope.

"What are you doing?" I bellowed. "What about me?"

"Don't worry," he shouted. "That fire's out of control."

His point being? "So what Dad? So are you."

"I've seen worse than this in combat," course he had to go on, didn't he? "And recently, let me tell you."

"Give me a break, let me come with you." I asked. He thought about this but not for long.

"It's a bit like being back at work. No, you stay here, son." He was pushing me away, again.

"I'm off, but you can get help. This time, I want more than prayers."

And he vanished.

Cheek! Giving me orders. I watched as the dinghy's tiny engine spluttered towards the beach and then took a huge breath in. Forgotten again, so what's new?

'Pull yourself together, Johnny boy,' that's what he'd say. I went to the two-way radio, my eyes focused on the Taverna. Luckily, my dad's boring but what I now saw was essential boat safety training came in. I easily sent the emergency message to the coastguard.

"My dad is trying to put a fire out," I yelled. "It's at the Taverna Dionysos," saying, "he really needs your help!"

The coastguard calmed me, "We're sending some fire fighters out right now," but he sounded miles away to me and what with their roads and them being so laid back, it could be too late for my dad.

'BANG!'

Another tall flame. Rubbish bin going up? I hope that's all it is. Whatever, it lit the beach and made me jump. The fire was growing. I hesitated not knowing what to do. Next thing, I was S.O.S.ing my mum. 'Please come quickly, Mum! We need you!'

For some reason, I was writing all this on the corner of the map. Plus three words I should have said earlier, 'I LOVE YOU.' Then I ripped it off and rolled it up into an empty plastic Fanta bottle that was lying about on deck finally, I chucked it overboard.

Mad. Don't ask me why.

Another crack! And again the flames roared higher. I couldn't just sit here. Time to make a difference. Luckily, adrenalin kicked in and gave me strength. And my mum's words were suddenly in my head. 'All that sport training is paying off, John.' I grabbed hold of a pair of flippers and goggles. I could do this, right? Putting them on, I dropped off the boat, catching my breath as I hit the water, then began swimming for all I was worth. The counting helped.

One, please don't let him die.

Two, please don't let him die.

Three, please don't let him die.

Four, five, six,.. Please don't let him die.

Each time I thought about my dad, it gave me a burst of energy. When I reached thirty, my knees scraped on the rocks and I was praying hard. Demetrius, I should have thought about Demetrius. I clambered heavily out of the water, exhausted. Flopping onto the sand, I threw off my suffocating goggles and flippers, wringing out the bottom of my baggy T-shirt. I ran up the beach and that's when the heat got to me. I put up an arm to shield my eyes. I could hardly hear a deafening sound of racing blood filled my head.

"Dad!" I yelled. "Dad! Where are you?"

I was desperate to find him but the sand scorched my skin. Glowing bits of blue wispy flamed debris marked the café boundary. Fans of roaring orange flames lapped around the kitchen door whilst black plastic sizzled off a buzzing sign. Scared or what? Yeah, I was scared but although the smoke got me, I kept searching. It felt as though I'd been looking for at least an hour.

I was tired out so I closed my eyes, quitting the nightmare in front of me. My body began to shake and my eyes were streaming with smoke. I rubbed them and it was as if the fire was in my eyes. "Ouch!" I yelped. Bad idea! I moved forward, coughing, wanting a cooler patch of sand to stop on. Again and again, I called, "Dad!" Thinking, "I can't lose you both!"

At last, amongst the pops and crackles filling the thick early morning sky came a faint groan, "Errr."

I took my T-shirt off and wrapped it round my nose and mouth heading for the sound, battling against the billows of putrid smoke. A gas cylinder was just in front of me and there, in the chaos, was my dad. He was face down protecting the char-grilled drunk. I had to get him out. Grabbing as much of his clothing as I could, I heaved for all I was worth. "Pull, pull!" came a strong voice inside me. I was not alone.

Then, sirens were coming quickly down the hill, mixed up with the sound of bells ringing. Was it three? I pulled harder, and slowly, we pulled my Dad and the drunk across the sand. This fantastic strength pulled with me, making it all doable. Even then, in the heat and confusion, I knew it was answered prayer. Carefully, I rolled them to the cool sands, by this time the yells were in Greek and they took over. Fire fighters with breathing equipment gave me some oxygen that made my head spin, saying, "Ise kala?" It sounded good to me, so I nodded. Later, Athena let me know it was 'Are you alright?'

"Efcharisto," I said, thanks. Like you do.

At last, we were safe. Thank God.

I relaxed into a warm blanket placed around my shoulders whilst a firefighter told me about Dad. "A brave man your dad, he probably saved the old man's life." Seeing my red toes curling, the firefighter got a wet cloth and put it under my feet. He told me that Dad needed to go to hospital. The paramedic had already given him a shot of painkillers through a drip but he needed some burns treating. The firefighter helped me stand and steadied me along, stepping over a rigid hose on the sand up to the ambulance. I would need to go, as well, to keep us together. Go to the main hospital, back at the capital. It was a good plan and he could see how I needed my dad, putting me in the front seat because the drunk had the other space in the back. The paramedics, who hardly had chance to talk to me, were passing manic messages. When I asked to see my dad, one said, "Your father's had some strong pain killers." I presumed they meant he was out of it.

Not until that night of the fire had I got that, even after the absolute worst things, day follows night with a welcome dawn. An odd owl hoot came in through the cracked open window. As the ambulance snaked up the hillside from the bay we left a spooky, dull cloud covering the sleepy shoreline. But ahead promised a warm new day. The driver was busy radioing ahead about us. In Greek, I picked up the words Steve and John White. He kept asking, "How are your feet, okay?"

I nodded, as you do, with an "efcharisto" thrown in. It made him smile in between checking on his mate in the rear-view. My dad was quiet. It worried me although the driver kept telling me he was ok, no problem. Believe it when I saw it! The noise from the drunk was a good sign. My feet started to throb again having moved the cold cloth to one of my hands, so I replaced it. At the hospital after an uncomfortable ride, one of the first things they did was to give me a bowl of cold water to plop my feet into. I splashed the water up my legs to my knees. Arr.. So much better.

For ages I kept pulling the blanket up over me then throwing it off. They gave me something to help lower my temperature and loads of water to drink. Amazingly, I dozed off sitting in a scruffy leather-look chair in the corridor, until a nurse rushed by with a wheelchair waking me. I grabbed at her tunic, "Have they finished treating him, how is my dad?" I was asking. With a baffled look, she pointed towards the reception. Kept in for observation overnight, I'd long since pulled my feet out the bowl of water. They seemed fine now, they did get me a bed but I didn't stay in it long. I shuffled along to the desk hutching up my blanket around me, "Yassou, my name is John White, I'm looking for Steve White." She knew who I was. The name board above my bed gave it away!

The receptionist's reply was fluent, "first of all are you feeling any better?"

I said, "Okay. But I need to find my dad," although my head

had started thumping.

She raised her eyebrows at me, questioning my ability to judge how I felt.

"Look, yes, I'm all right."

Why I bothered though, she still ignored me. "I need to find a doctor to check you over, go back to your bed." How rude!

Annoyingly clicking her nails on the computer she went, "You'll have plenty of time to see your father, he's only around the corner," then she carried on gabbling on the phone.

So I went for a wander and leant towards the front door to catch a breath of fresh air. There, I was totally gob-smacked by a new fire. Only it was harmless this time, a natural one, rising up from the sea. So that's what Dad had been raving about. The sunrise. Then, I felt I was being watched.

"The best way you can help your dad, is to look after yourself," Athena was going; I didn't even see where she'd come from. "My, hero! But what was your dad thinking of? He was in no fit state to try saving our place, you should've told me." Too much information! And what was it I should have told her exactly? But I couldn't faze her, she was on a roll. "The hospital told me on the phone that your dad's had some burns treated and he's got a cough but he's been lucky, compared to the poor drunk. I had to get down here to make sure you were okay." She'd got a lift with her uncle in his taxi.

My face scrunched up at her outburst. Holding my head, I was thinking I'd soon have no one left at this rate! Did she mean that my life was spiralling out of control or that she was quite fit? Who knows! Before I had chance to say she butted in, "You both need to rest a while. If you want, you can stay at our house. Do as Athena says, I'm not named after the goddess of wisdom for nothing, you know."

First, I had to face him. "Yeah, after I've seen my dad I'll be glad to be out of here, I could give you a hand at the café," I decided. But she shook her head. No such luck, they made me wait to see the doctor who was putting cream on my feet and hand when he let me have the remainder of the tube, along with a prescription. What? All a bit over the top but I'd do whatever, to get them off my case. Some tablets needed collecting from the pharmacy; Athena went off to get them for me. Eventually, they let me know the ward where my dad was. It was a burns bay!

4. BIRTHDAY IN HOSPITAL

My knees buckled but I followed the blue line on the floor, to the burns bay. This was where dad was, sitting propped up in bed. And there I was, visiting another hospital ward in another country. So different but with just the same foul smell, only this time it was my dad, a complete nightmare. I couldn't stand it and my heart beat scarily till I got a grip. The ward seemed stuffy despite a fan buzzing away in the corner. As I got closer he watched me flicking my hand where the cream was stinging.

"Johnny my lad, how are you?" the drip-line pulled him back as he reached towards me.

I just shook my head, lingering at the end of the bed and going from one foot to another while trying to decode his clinical notes. I wanted to fly at him and hug him at the same time. It was worth checking that I wasn't about to become an orphan, first. Useless, they were written with letters like triangles! I had to take a load off. All this, after having sworn I'd never to set foot in another hospital again!

Eventually, I lied, "I'm not bad," then, "well let's put it this way, I'm doing much better than you, Dad! I'll live, anyhow." I burst into nervous laughter crossing my arms, "But what are we gonna do with you?" Shrugging heavily I asked, "What do these tatty notes say anyhow?"

Dad felt his long stubble, obviously aggravating him, "I'm

alright, nothing a few days rest won't sort out, don't worry about me son. It all came to a bit of a head. I was totally paralysed, not like me... But I'm really sorry to bring you here; after all we've been through."

"Oh yeah, what a bummer. I wasn't too chuffed coming in here either but I suppose you did tell me not to follow," I sighed. It felt like days not hours since he swam away from our catamaran. Was he attention seeking? I'd seen it before, with the lads who skipped school, bored so they played up.

"Anyway, Happy Birthday, I meant to say... Sixteen at last! How does that feel?"

I forced a smile, "Oh, yeah. Thanks a lot. No need to panic, I've got to wait a whole year before I can drive. How wrong is that?" I joked, fiddling with the sheet scrunched at the end of his bed.

Going on he said, "My problem is I still think I'm on active duty, I should have left it to the local lads to deal with the fire."

"Do you think?" I said, sarcastically. "Don't worry about it, Rambo, next time I might just take a rain check myself." No signs of presents, I continued scanning the ward for exits.

"No son really, I've got to think of us more now," wriggling he continued, "it's just so hard to stop yourself, when you've had all the training."

My eyebrows lifted, "I'm sure," how sincere I sounded, not! When would he get over himself?

He pulled up to sit up on the bed, fidgeting, "Well, here we are, with all the time in the world. Now might be the right time to let each other know how we actually feel. It's really hard mate, so if you like I'll start?" He looked up staring straight into my eyes. Eeeeek!

All I said was, "I don't know whether I've had enough of this kinda fun, for one day." What I wanted to say was, "Great!" but feeling jumpy I turned to see what was happening behind me, as a new patient was brought in. Then I rambled on, "Guess what? Last night you kept me up late enough to see one of those sunrises you've been on about. To do it properly you need company, I think." He grinned back at me but I kept on with the small talk, "The N.H.S. is brilliant compared to this isn't it? Mum wouldn't think much..." I'd let slip.

He gasped, "But John, the only way you could tell her is via the answer phone, that's as good as you'll get," stretching forward with wide eyes.

"Do you know that'll be just what I'll have to do then, won't it?" I snapped, gulping.

"How did we ever get in such a state, with us being so close? You know I'm here for you, don't you?" A bit like our cat licking his wounds, I listened closely. Was he for real? I eyeballed him. But then a stupid nurse barged in, telling about some visitor and totally messing up.

I kicked the bed leg as I got up and there was a familiar voice, "Who've we got here then?" He started to whistle happy birthday. Next he was giving me this hug.

"It's Paul, great to see you." I looked at Dad.

"Too right John, I wouldn't miss your sixteenth for anything. Your dad made the headlines at home, well, a hotmail message. You could still make the Melton Times I bet; *Local Hero Saves the Day*, but it'll take them a week or two!" He made me laugh.

Dad didn't answer. He just threw Paul a dagger of a look.

"How're you both feeling?" Paul asked, sensing awkwardness.

I ached but the sight of this long wrapped parcel cheered me up, "Well I was feeling better till you made it to a party! Thanks for the present. What is it?" I thought about how retail therapy worked for me.

"A little bird told me you needed some decent fishing tackle. Something about you only being able to catch tiddlers!" He kidded.

"I don't know where you get your information from but the rod's classic, thanks." I smiled at him, unpacking the latest plastic folded type. It didn't seem right; normally I'd wait for Mum before opening anything. "You may as well meet Athena while you're here. She's my friend and I might be going to stay with her for a while if…"

"Yeah, okay then I'll come back and sit with your dad a while," he said, seeing I was not happy.

"Dad I'm off to Athena's then, I'll catch you later, when you know what you're doing."

"Make sure you keep your mobile on, they may let me come back on the boat," then, "okay, Paul, I'm not going anywhere for the moment." I could tell by his moustache twiddling, he was getting a bit wound up. I remember he had the same look when Mum had told him that she loved this 'Jesus' more than him, spitting he was. I suppose she had that one coming. Even though she'd explained!

As we walked Paul cheered me up telling me this joke about a bloke shipwrecked on a desert island. He went on about this old guy praying to be saved but when a passing ship saw him and asked him to climb aboard and a helicopter landed to fetch him, then a lifeboat called for him he said, 'No thanks,' because he was waiting for God. Paul was belly laughing as he said that at the pearly gates God told the twit why he'd died, 'Well, I sent two boats and a helicopter. What more did you want?"

I laughed. He still had his arm around me as we got to the info desk, "Let's introduce you to Athena."

"Slow down a bit. Before all that, how's Steve really?" he blocked me.

"You'll find out for yourself in a minute, he'll be more chatty with me out of the way."

"I know, it's just I wanted to see if he's talking much about your mum. Does he say he misses her?"

"You're kidding, he never even mentions her. Something about he's had the right training for dealing with these kinda things! I give up, cos recently I've stopped trying to bring her into the conversation. That's where Athena's been really great. The Greeks never stop talking. Come with me to meet her, she's at the info desk."

"Alright, if you're heading off I'll catch you again later, shall

I?" He said.

"Yeah, Athena will let you have her address, Paul." I hobbled up seeing her drop the magazine back onto the table. She watched us come closer, eyebrows lifted curious about the gift.

"Look who's come all the way from England to see us, it's Uncle Paul. Can you remember, I told you he was an alright kinda guy?" I watched her nod, "Well, he bought me a new fishing rod."

"Hello, John's Uncle Paul. Yes, you told me!" She smiled.

"I'm pleased to meet you, Athena. Any friend of John's is a friend of mine." They chatted, me busy listening to a nurse I found out too late to stop Paul saying, "It seems I owe you one, young lady. John tells me you've been a good friend to him and his dad since they lost Annie."

"Yes, err, no problem." She hesitated. We heard a car horn coming from the main entrance.

"Anyway, that's our taxi waiting, we'll see you back at Kindos Bay later at the Taverna." Embarrassed, I pulled Athena with me towards the door. "Please come and have something to eat with us. The food's absolutely delicious. Ring my mobile if you want Athena's Uncle to pick you up." Forgetting what I was doing.

Athena interrupted me slowing me down, "Sorry, Paul we'll actually be up at the house but all the same, do come up." Athena put me right. I made a gesture for her to write on a leaflet I had taken out of my shorts pocket, asking, "Can you write the address down for Paul, please?" She grabbed a pen off the info desk and did it for him.

"Bye, Paul and thanks." I sighed.

5. PAUL ON INTERNATIONAL RESCUE

"I dread to think what Dad will tell Paul," I cringed. "He went on to me about, 'A real storm can change the world beyond compare,' earlier. So heavy! I don't know whether he was comparing it to the sea, our lives or what. You got any idea, Athena?"

"Oh, John, I'm not sure," she went along with me.

"It beats me, not a clue! Maybe Paul can find out about what's going on in my Dad's head." I sighed.

"I hope so," she nodded.

My attempt to cover up wasn't fooling her. Athena just wouldn't leave it. She gave me her wide eyed look, asking, "You gonna tell me about Annie, or what?"

Looking away I tried to brush it off before we got in the car, "She was just…" I shrugged.

Too late, Athena had got it, "She was just your mum, John, wasn't she? I wondered when you'd let me in on the secret."

"Well, I …"

Luckily, she interrupted. "I've known since early this morning. We were clearing up at the beach when I found your message in a bottle. Sorry I read it before I realised, it was a bit weird so I asked my dad if he knew anything. Don't worry I lobbed it back into the sea, off the pier.

"No way! I'm the one who's sorry, you didn't need to know this." I wriggled.

"Don't be silly. My dad told me after Steve was all choked up a few nights ago, well, then he let it slip out. About your mum being dead. We should know how much you two have got happening in your lives," she told me. "Otherwise, how else could we help? Well, apart from cook your dinner, that is!" My mum has a meal on for everyone at home. That's what she does in a crisis, feed everyone!" She threw me one of her life saving smiles. Making everything sound so simple.

Her uncle chirped up, having manoeuvred out of the car parking space. "Yassou, okay? That sounds a good idea, dinner. It will make you feel so much better."

"Yassou, you're the best, Alec. I can't wait and hopefully, my uncle Paul is going to join us later. When he's cheered my dad up, that is. You know, luckily, my dad doesn't look that bad, easy for me to say!"

"No, I hear it was down to you that Steve's still here. You found him pinned down, didn't you? Most of us would have waited for help. You finished the job your dad started, moving those gas cylinders. A brave lad, I'd say."

Uneasily, I shifted around in my seat, not enjoying the fuss. I certainly didn't do it for my reputation. In fact, more like for self preservation- purely selfish reasons. Everyone deserves at least one parent, don't they? I suppose bizarrely, it showed that I actually cared about my dad. We just drove straight on by the café, albeit slowly. There was a massive clean-up going on. The whole community seemed to have turned out. It must be fantastic, I thought, to have all those friends. From the road I could see the place was in a right mess. They had dragged away most of the scorched partition and canopy which was all now heaped on the rubbish cart. Ready to go.

"Wow, that looks bad," I gulped.

Athena picked me up, "Look, you've done your bit, they'll soon get it fixed with a lick of paint," being completely chilled about it.

It looked a write off to me! Alec drove on and up the dust track that led to their farmhouse. I was stressing about leaving Paul with Dad, really hoping he wasn't winding him up, even more!

Athena went off to make us drinks. The late afternoon sun was quite hot. I swung back and forth on a hammock attached to a pair of olive trees. Was this like heaven, or what? But then I had to come under the canopy when I felt like puking, being such a lightweight! She pulled up a plastic chair and passed me the cold can.

I just wanted to sleep, to be honest. Instead, like a fool I let my eyes fill up and it all spilt out, "My mum wasn't supposed to die. She'd had one cancer already. She'd fought and won, was getting better so I thought. They'd given her this boob operation and she was taking drugs for the next 5 years. Sorted! Supposed to be but...not! My poor old Annie, Jane, White. In and out of hospital, then in remission, she just accepted her days were numbered. Not me. Cos it was totally NOT FAIR!" That bit came out too loud. "You see why I hate hospitals? She was meant to be getting better. Those doctors let her down when I still needed her." Oh, no! Did I actually say all that? Talk about sad.

Athena just watched, listening. Eventually, she asked, "When was all this, when did she die?"

That's what I loved about her, straight to the point. "Huh? Oh, it was back in July. She died at the end of July." I felt this twisted gut, tighten in my stomach. "A proper rainy day. Der! I didn't even realise she was ill again till about a week before it actually happened. And nobody wanted to worry me, having just finished my exams. They let me be. So called, protected me." I swept the sweat from my head. "Oh, I really wish they had told me earlier. The clue was she was having parties and filled our house with friends. Stupidly, I read that as a good sign. Thinking she was feeling more up for it, seeing friends and stuff. So I let her get on with it, thinking she was okay. Can you believe that I could be so stupid?" I looked down.

Athena shook her head. "It's not your fault, they should have told you."

"I felt such a plonker. Anyway... she refused any more hospitals. No more treatment, just to make the best of her time left. I get it now. But the trouble is I've never seen anyone die before. And she was still smiling, that's what got me. She went to the hospice in the day and came home with a nurse at night. I got used to that. Then her lungs packed up, she had pneumonia. Still acting normal and chilling with my friends, I was. Clueless! That's why it hit me like a freight train. And when it happened, I ran and ran. I had to get away. You see, I hadn't even said goodbye to her. Not properly. Paul found me in the woods later. My dad completely flipped. He was not happy."

Waiting she said, "It must have been awful! When my gran died last year, we kept her at home for a couple of days in her brass-handled coffin. That made it easy to believe. All us grand-kids came to see her lying in her best clothes, peaceful."

"Really?" Was that a good idea? I was thinking about that one. Then, I sighed. "I still really miss her. You'd expect me to miss me mum, though. I'm all right till some idiot says 'the good die young' and that creases me. Let's change the subject, shall we? I had a go on your hammock, by the way. And I've been eyeing up your moped but in my state, I'd better leave it well alone cos my history's not good on them. Lately, I've been doing dodgy things until Ben sorted me and covered for me."

"Honestly, I don't mind." She moved up close.

"At least they say she's in a better place, now. And it wasn't all bad. Some days were great. Behind mum's hospice, there's this cool farmyard with a giant haystack. In the centre of the barn roof hangs a fantastic, tug-o-war like rope, with an old tyre attached. I've spent many Saturdays swinging on it with the manager's son, Ross. Like big kids! We'd go indoors to get some grub, then climb up and do it again. Until I forgot why mum was there. So, don't feel too sorry for me."

"Okay, then." She laughed.

I heard car doors banging. "Was Paul here already in the taxi?" I asked myself.

Sure enough, my uncle came through the gate with Alec. They chatted before Paul joined us. Athena made him welcome by fetching him a nice cold orange juice. While she was there, Paul started giving me all this out-of-order heavy stuff.

"It's been three months now. It's time you admitted it. You and your dad are as bad as each other," he nagged.

"One thing you're forgetting, Paul. I believed God would heal my mum." I said, defensively.

"I don't understand why certain things have to happen, either," Paul replied in the only way he knew how. "Some things are meant to be. Remember what happened to Paul when he sailed from Crete?"

"No," I said, not bothered.

Opening up his bible, "The sailors thought it was the right thing to do because a soldier put pressure on them. Paul warned them not to get sucked in. The results were scary, a shipwreck. What they should have realised was that their trip had been getting rougher for a reason. It was to divert them back onto the right path. Instead of rethinking their route, accepting the future, they just kept on with their agenda straight into a raging storm."

"Great!" I felt confused. "So what's his sorry act got to do with me?" I said.

"Your mum gave a good fight but God had something better for her and I know your mum will be pain free in heaven." He looked seriously at me. "More importantly, so did your mum!"

"Yeah, yeah!" I sighed.

"Well, at least start realizing your mum's not coming back. You'll have to wait to see her in eternity, someday." He was trying to help, so he went on, "You've had a slight detour with this Greek trip but now it's the time to face the truth. Not alone. I'm totally here for you. Life goes on. And your dad's getting better, so you'll get another chance with him. You two need to pull together. Come home - that's my advice. Lots of people want to help you both because they loved your mum. Let them do this for her, please." He took a breath then asked, "Are you ready to pick up the pieces?"

"I suppose so, but its Dad you need to talk to, not me," I told him.

"That's sorted then! Your dad's agreed to you both having some help, while he makes his recovery from the burns. It'll do you good to see Ben and your other mates; I bet you're missing them."He put his arm round me, squeezing, "You know, youth club's been rubbish without you." Laughing, as he saw what was coming.

Clever Athena had taken her time but it was worth it. She only came out with a huge chocolate cake, with candles in. Bonus! And then Paul lit them. After I'd blown them out, without making a wish, she handed us a decent slab asking me, "And when exactly were you going to let me know it was your birthday? Or as we say, Xronia Polla."

She was brilliant. "Honestly, I forgot." I spat between chewing this gooey, cocoa dream cake. "I've just had too much going on." I gave her my cutest grin.

Smiling back she asked, "How long will your dad be in hospital for John, do you know?"

Paul spoke for me, "He'll be out in the next day or two, then we can get some flights home." My mouth being completely crammed with cake, I kept it shut. Athena looked amazed for a moment.

Later, we ate a lovely meal of lamb with weird green bits, Athena's mum had made. Like peppery, it was hot! It was to thank all the helpers. Throughout this meal her family shook my good hand, as they came up from the beach. After eating, Paul made his excuses to go back to the hospital, via the boat to collect our laptop. He was going to start a flight search on the net. Him hoping for a wired system in the hospital, slim chance! Also, he was visiting the drunk to see how his burns were doing. I limped up to bed feeling exhausted not long after Paul went. A bad thought flashed across my mind, did Dad want to die in the fire and that's why he wasn't that crazy about waking up in the hospital? But after a couple of paracetamol and a swig of water, I was past caring.

Next afternoon, after I'd slept like a baby, I wandered down to see how the café repairs were going. Black dust coated everything. It all had to be cleaned off. Mop and buckets with manic scrubbing seemed to be doing the trick. Being a bit sore, it cheered me up to see our mog begging at one of the tables. He hadn't got that the café was closed. At least he'd survived. Later, Dad was allowed out of hospital quietly spending the night on the boat with Paul. I just chilled at Athena's. After our day's rest, the café Dionysos threw us a fantastic, farewell feast. It was a barbeque with Greek salad all pre-prepared and brought down from the house. There were these aptly draped tablecloths to hide the damage but it was okay because I got to sit with Athena. We talked about keeping in touch on facebook. We ate by candlelight, which was awesome. And she made me laugh guessing how far the message in a bottle might get to, in the sea. She was talking miles- to the Suez Canal. As if!

When I said, "You never know!" She mentioned something about adding a paper napkin from the café, into the bottle. It had her address on. Still, it was special and I wondered why we had to head home. I managed a hug from Athena, but got one from most of her family too! Arrr... That was a right pain. Then we three collapsed on the boat for a final night.

Next morning, before we needed to leave for our flight, I ended up climbing the steep path to see the cheeky Madonna statue. Watching my step on the narrow path, it took a while to get my breath back. Climbing the steps, two at a time, the views were incredible. I wanted to shout out to hear the echo but I bottled it. Looking straight up from various places on the hill, sometimes, the statue was completely hidden. For me she was like a magnet, cold stone on one side but her smile was warm, on the other. Spooky. But like Mum, she left you something good. Funny, I hadn't thought about that. About what Annie had left me, before. Then I thought, the thing that Mum left me it was...

HOPE.

These deep ideas were interrupted by this annoying,

coughing noise.

"I found you," my dad said, out of breath. It helped him knowing where to look. Since he knew me a bit better, this time I went AWOL.

So without taking my eyes off the statue, "Huh," is all I said.

"What have you come up here for?" Waiting he went on, "We've really got to be in the taxi, cruising for the airport, in the next hour."

"No problem. Is it an optical illusion or is my mind playing tricks on me? First you see her, then you don't!" That's what I asked my dad when he calmed down, following me, all that way up there. Quite impressive, for an old dude! His training, he'd say. It was about time I remembered my training- what Mum taught me. Now that was quite a lot!

He was getting used to my runners not taking them personally, just letting me off, saying, "I never know what you're playing at, so why should I have a clue about some statue? The older I get the less I understand, just don't ask!" He joined me standing back giving her the once-over. Our touristy bit done, we could at last think of going home. Dad explained that Athena's dad had agreed to organize our boat pick up and settle the account. Demetrius insisted, saying it was the least he could do. So with that sorted, there was nothing to stop us heading back. I felt a bit panicky, again.

Us three travelled back to the East Midlands, Paul, my dad and me who'd done some growing up. The flight was okay, spoilt by a sad, chick flick but the finger licking food made up for it. Dad made this big speech about, 'Things are going to change,' as we touched down at the Nottingham airport. Bring it on! I thought I could cope with that.

6. NOTHING TO LOOK FORWARD TO BACK HOME

Things were happening, after the return flight. The countryside looked so green without the lush, Greek Island colours. And the fields had pencil-drawn perfect boundaries; I was surprised at how neat it looked as we drove back from Nottingham. Rattling along in Paul's primer splattered fiesta, we clunked over the canal bridge. Back in our village I sank down in my seat. A plant stall was begging for another random cause. My carefree stuff dropped away for those chains, restraining my breathing. Slowly does it. Don't panic, I said to myself biting my lip.

As we came past the park I cranked my neck out to see if I could spot a 360 kick flip, being done on the half pipe. No such luck, down to the rain. My mates had run for cover in the youth shelter, a cloud of smoke gave them away. They should have squeezed in the corner shop. That would have been much healthier. The lovely, tempting corner shop that oozed out wicked bacon smells. "Are we stopping for a buttie or what?" I asked. I thought it was worth a try. No such luck.

"Your Aunt Joan would go mad if you missed her homecoming lunch, it won't hurt you to wait a couple of hours," Dad told me and I couldn't believe that Paul didn't even slow down. They should give me a break.

"Great, something healthy with salad, no-doubt! Terrific,

can't wait." I moaned, holding my head in my hands until we pulled up onto the drive. I half expected a 'For Sale' sign up. He was good enough not to tell me. Our front garden had gone kind of monochrome, the lawn was set-aside, at its best. But that was okay because it was no longer my job. Dad was chief mower now he was sticking around a bit more. Things looked the same but different. A bit like me. Boris, next door's mangy mog rushed up as I jumped out the back of the nail. I burst in the side door letting my backpack clank heavily on the kitchen table, which made Joan's cheesy smile drop.

I was in trouble already!

Tea, cokes and sandwiches filled the tabletop she'd cleared. I grabbed a can and emptied a pack of crisps down my neck. I wanted space. I couldn't be doing with those cards through in the lounge yet. I needed air. And Joan kept tidying. So I leant down, grabbed my skateboard from the utility room, gassed by a bitter whiff of Dad's putrid pumps and escaped outside.

"Where do you think you're off to?" came a daft question from Dad with the suitcases. I just ignored him, feeling the need to launch myself from my practice jump, out the back. Like everything was normal, I was counting on an adrenalin rush blasting away the crap. Then texting Ben to come save me, I slammed hard into next doors fence. I stayed there waiting. Nothing. Next time I'll try harder but there were too many weeds clogging the path, to get any decent kind of speed up. Wounded! So I moved towards the cat noticing on our washing line this ridiculous piny peg holder. I lobbed a mouldy tennis ball from the back lawn, hard against it. Bingo! It smelt rancid.

Dad must have picked up that I was stressed because before long Joan was out the door, waving bye. And I heard Paul talking as he walked to the car, as well. All I wanted was normal. The house wasn't right, just a random house not our home any more. Having got rid of Joan, from Paul came this almighty spiel… It was meant to help, I know. He meant well. But we were exhausted from travelling and the thought of facing the future was terrifying. Dad's worried face didn't deter Paul. Definitely a man with a mission, he threw in, "I'll say it now because it won't be easier tomorrow." Cringe. Poor Dad!

Paul kept on at him about the five stages of mourning. The good news was he seemed to have covered three - *denial, anger and depression*, without realising! The *bargaining* part he was coming up to, then he could get on with the most important part *acceptance*, to fit cosily into this scheme. I found my eyes glaze over and felt sad that Paul had to give it to him like this. Dad, less apologetic said, "You know Paul, I'm sure in a few days all that will make sense but for today, it's going straight over my head!"

Picking up on Paul's disappointed look, I continued, "Why don't we get together to go bowling in the week, when you can run it by us again?" Phew! It worked. He just hugged us and said he would keep praying. Next, his car door slammed. Finally, Dad and I were alone. I went inside. All around us was Mum. Her coat was on the back of the dining room chair and her hairbrush on the mantle piece. And those cards and photos! All Paul had just said took me back to the Thanksgiving service. I tasted salty tears as my body felt heavy. I gulped. I couldn't stop myself going back, remembering. There I was, in the church, with the all too familiar blurring. But then, as I blinked to clear it, the coffin wafted by and my eyes stung, full of burning ice. How I held myself together I don't know. My ears thumped with the pounding in my chest. I did well not to fall, as my whole blood supply sank to my feet.

I remember the timing. It was perfect. Timing. Someone grabbed hold of my hand, I've no idea who. I so wanted it to be Mum. And I was all right until they did that blessing bit, at the end. That made me dissolve. More likely, it was God who held me by the hand.

Back to our lounge, on the mantelpiece next to the cards I found the order of service. I rubbed the dust off on my sleeve. Mum would have hated that. And there was a lovely fresh picture of my mum, grinning. When she could only have been eighteen. When she was so alive. I moved to the back page and read those words we said together, back at the funeral:

> *Annie*
> *May the road rise up to meet you,*
> *May the wind be always at your back,*
> *May the sunshine warm your face,*
> *May the rains fall soft upon your fields.*
> *And until we meet again,*

May God hold you in the hollow of his hand.

It pierced me like a blade. Dad saw what I had in my hand and touched my arm as if to say, 'I know.' All I could think of was, if God chose to hold my hand through the service, then he would definitely hold Mum safely in his hand, when so many of us asked for it.

I wiped my eyes, turning away. Dealing with it.

Then Dad said, "Remember Joan read that note from Mum. The one that said that Annie wasn't scared to die and that we must try to get over it. Apparently it's from the bible, here look I've got a copy, "You will weep and mourn," he started to read it to me, "but your grief will turn to joy… and no one will take (it) away." When he looked up his eyes were watering. But I was well impressed. Then for some reason, I went sad again thinking, how could I ever have joy from Mum's death? From deep down, how random, this anger came up and I screamed. "But she was good and didn't deserve to die! She had so much left to do. Like, be my mum! It's not fair. How could this happen?"

Dad replied, "I don't know. Sorry, son. I'm as shocked as you are that she's gone. I just really need to know when the joy part will kick in, that your mum promised. I'm hanging onto that bit." He tried to smile and cheer me up.

He was wrong. It wasn't Mum who promised. She was just telling us about God's promise. So I mustn't be sad, I hoped this time was just like a black cloud blowing over our lives. Which, eventually would move away. That's what it meant in the note. I couldn't see us coming out of it for ages at the rate we were going.

Then I remembered what they'd said at the hospice. Something about, when we were ready, they'd help us. Next time I saw Paul, I might ask what they might do to us. He went in there to help out with things. He knew what they did. I felt my cheeks go red just thinking about it, for me! Awful! The thought of telling anyone else, like a big wuzz! When Mum was there, it was different because she needed it. I'd gone to see what she got up to, lots of relaxation stuff and treats, like her hair done and hand massages. They did lots of crafts and ate huge cakes. There were these scary, therapy rooms. Some stuff wasn't that bad but I knew she did her crying there, to save us hearing her. I loved her. They showed her love, I owed them big time for that. Them being there for her.

Before I could stop it, I felt myself go. Out of control. I was in that awful state of girly wailing. My body rattled. I had to let it all drain away. Snot streamed mixed into a tear river and was caught on my sleeve. Not a pretty sight or sound. But it had to happen. I thumped the cushion. Dad was just there next to me, slumped on the settee. I couldn't see him beyond my tears but before he enveloped me I knew he was there. He was rattling, too! There was this muffled, "Don't get upset!" then he said, "Please don't because you'll set me off again." Too late! When I picked up on the 'again,' I reached out for him. And I held him, like I was never going to let him go.

His pain had to come out, too. A blubbering mass we melted

together.

Safe. In our lounge.

The words, 'I'm sorry,' came out of Dad's mouth. Why did he need to say that? 'Sorry.' But it somehow made a difference. That night Dad turned off the house phone, we locked the doors and just kept close. He made me toast. He told me that we were going to be all right! Then we slept for hours, him on the armchair and me on the settee. Fast asleep until morning.

When I woke up my head was thumping. Dad's eyes looked as though he'd been in a boxing match and he ached all over. Strange but true, I felt better though. Crazy! By the way Dad was, I knew he felt a bit better, too. Then we just slobbed-out all that day. I ignored my text message bleep. Quite hard to do, so I just let the battery run down. The washer was going with an emergency load, so we were in old tracky bottoms and ridiculous T-shirts. I even put Ben off coming round. We needed to be just us two and keep the safe bit. We were taking in the last lung-fulls of Mum, before we had to start to let her go. Together. The photo albums came out and we started to cry but this time there were laughs in there too. And it was under control, again. A relief!

The next day I saw it had been Athena, texting. I should have let her know we were back safe. She was letting me know we'd missed a great opening party at the Taverna. She asked me to fill her in on all my news and ended, 'misin u aoys'. That was nice, the angel on your shoulder bit. Paul was reminding us, on the phone, that it was the bowling night. We were ready for getting out. The curtains needed drawing to let a bit of light in. Dad tried to wheedle out of bowling, with some excuse making out Paul and I would have a better time without him. Not so easy. I knew we had to do this. So I crept round him till he had no choice, giving him the 'best dad in the world' routine! I couldn't have known how much it was going to hurt. It started off an innocent game of glow bowling. Ha-ha! Embarrassing. The lights somehow set him off thinking, back to the night of the fire. Then my dad was upset, again. All I did was go to the loo, when I came back there were these red rings around his eyes.

I heard my dad say something about 'not knowing what to say to him.' I wondered if he was talking about me. Rubbing his face he went on, "It was one of the few times in my life I've felt completely helpless. When my Annie died." I saw him shove a copy of Mum's letter back in his pocket. That was good, him asking questions.

It made a lump come to my throat. Paul just kept listening. I looked at my macho dad and saw his vulnerable side. Apart from the obvious raw hand and wearing bowling shoes a size up to account of his sore toes. He stopped talking whilst he took his go and still he got a strike, due to the serious power behind the ball. I glanced Paul's way giving him the 'at last' look! Dad carried on saying, "But then it happened again. This time it was on the beach I knew it wasn't fear that did it but a build-up of everything. I ended up face down and paralyzed. Confronted by this drunk who needed my help and all I could think of was Annie and how I couldn't help her,"

Dad said.

Paul butted in, "Neither of these things were your fault, you know."

And then everything seemed okay, for a minute. It was like someone took a huge weight off his shoulders. I had a go at bowling and got a spare, not bad! Good job it was my left hand that was not right.

"You don't have to be Rambo all the time, you know Dad," is all I could think of to say. He winked at me.

Paul had been quiet listening carefully to Steve, "You ought to read the story of Daniel one day. He had a similar experience but felt he'd been helped by SOMEONE."

He shrugged, "There was something strange happened on the beach, that's for sure. Don't ask me what."

I knew what I thought and so said it, without really thinking, "Don't you think it could have been Mum trying to help us out?" I could see I'd blown the conversation when Paul put me right. His look of concern went from me to my dad.

"Your know your mum had gone by then though, Johnny. But it may well have been the same person from whom she got her strength, you know, Jesus." Dad had gone on the defensive by now. Then he started walking. He reminded me of how I used to be!

"Sorry," I said to Paul chasing after him, "he was starting to listen as well!"

I found Dad in his BMW fiddling with the C.D. player. From his frosty face, I took it that his defence shield was back up.

He looked miles away. I heard him threatening to go back to Greece, for some peace. Who was the child here? We didn't talk on the way home. He needed to get a life. I wondered whether Paul would carry on playing with some random bowlers, never wanting to waste an opportunity. And being tight.

When we got back in, I gave him who must be obeyed, some space. I was trying to say something to help before losing myself outside, "Dad, you're not thinking of going back on active duty, are you?" I made sure he was listening before digging a bigger hole for myself, "It sounds daft but I always thought you'd die first, well before Mum. I've dreamt of the dreaded knock on the door, from some Navy stiff in a suit." It probably made him worse, adding, "Hello, actually a nightmare."

It certainly got a response, "Oh, sorry to disappoint!" He winced. I hadn't meant to kick him when he was down. But that's how it must have felt, from the look on his face. I was just stating a fact, at the wrong time, maybe. He quickly came back at me, "For your information, when you were knocking around with that Joe lad, I thought it might be you to cop it, before either of us wrinklies." One to him! He could see how shocked I was and went on, "Yes, I remember worrying about Joe's drug-using habit, rubbing off on you. That wasn't so long ago, either!" I never even thought of that.

So we had both been well off track. This dreaded worry call of duty, getting us both in hot water. Okay, he was talking about Joe, who even forgot to use an alias for a tag, on the park. Yeah, right. That got him the job of a huge clean up. I always thought of him as pathetic. As if I'd copy what he did!

"Your gentle innocent mum was taken first. Who would have thought, with her clean living, she'd be the one to cop it? It beats me."

"Huh," I said but 'God works in mysterious ways,' went through my head. Easy for me to say but not right for my dad, now. I'd done enough damage for one day and didn't want to press any more of his buttons. "I'm off to see Ben for a bit. Tell you what, Dad, shall we make a deal? Let's not push our luck doing anything risky, for the time being. There must be some middle ground, here. So we don't have to worry about one another. Okay with you?"

"Deal," he lifted his hand to give me a high five. Then I turned away but as I slipped out the door he yelled, "But I'll still wait up for you!" That's the kind of thing my mum would have done. Did he care more or he was he taking on some of her jobs? He was all or nothing. At the minute he was getting excited by, the all bit. Okay with me.

When I rolled up at the park, Ben landed his scooter right next to me.

"What's up, John?" He asked, as if there was no stress. I knew he was here all the time, down to it all happening in his house. They went from one crisis to another and with five kids, they just keep occurring. But somehow they cope. They have to.

"I'm alright," and I was starting to believe it. Dad's opening up was the start. I was being normal. There was this shoving going off at the top of the ramp. I ignored it, as it involved Jez. Jez was this small fry with several issues. A weirdo is what they called him because they didn't know. I never felt the need to shut him up. I knew to back right off, give him his space and then he was okay. Ben forgot to give him a break for some reason, giving him some serious verbal.

As Ben raced past I asked, "What's Jez's problem tonight?"

"Ignore him; you know what he's like, big gob. I had to spell it out to him, why he should shut it, about your Ma," Ben said, getting his breath back.

"It's okay. I'll talk to him, leave it Ben." I didn't want him confused because he'd be worse. So I spent the next few minutes trying to catch him on my scooter. He skulked around thinking Ben would batter him for being in my face but I convinced him that he was okay with it.

We both stopped at the top of the ramp, the wind in our faces and annoying hair. It had been well blowy and the sky was whipping up with swirling clouds. There were these grey and purple monsters bounding across, with long white tails. I sat staring. "Have you seen the sky?" I asked Jez. "It's awesome!" He looked back, sheepish with a 'what's the point' look?'

"You're bang on, Jez. I'm not all right. I miss my mum. Well, my mum's up there now," I said, pointing to the sky. "But she's not in that angry grey bit. She told me she was happy to go, she'd had enough pain. She's resting up there with God, where there's no more agro, on one of those fluffy clouds. So you see, it's great for her up there," I said, smiling.

Jez surprised me by smiling back. My explanation had worked, "That's cool," is all I got out of him, as he slipped down the ramp on his board. He was leaving me thinking. Thinking about my life without her. It was all right that God had a place for Mum but what about my place? When I'd explained it to Jez it seemed real, my problem was believing for myself. I thought I'd text Athena for help. It must have been the wrong time. She didn't come back to me. Ben managed to wear me out, not letting me head back home until I'd set a new personal best on the half-pipe. And I was crashing a lot, which got me aching with the light going.

"See you tomorrow, mate," Ben shouted scootering off. But Jez kept following me.

I crept in not wanting to hassle my dad. But his head popped up from the sofa, "Can I get you lads a drink before you go up?" He asked. Now, he was trying too hard.

"You're alright, I've got it," grabbing two cokes from the fridge. "What about you?" I asked.

"I'm caffeined up for now, cheers," he said, followed by, "I see you've had a good night," giving me the once over. There was a dried bloody mess on my right knee that I tried to rub off. "And you're the one who made a deal, heh?" Giving me a wide-eyed look, he smiled, "Can I clean that up for you?" Still trying really hard.

"I'm gonna jump in the shower before I crash so that should see to it, thanks Dad." I brushed against him on my way upstairs, letting him know he'd got my vote. I needed to sleep tonight. I needed that deep sleep, where dreams can't interrupt you and you feel safe. I could hear my dad talking downstairs. Annoying, but I couldn't be asked to get details. If I left Jez alone long enough he'd soon be snoozing. The shower warmed me up so that's when I flopped onto my bed, I just sank into the quilt not moving until morning. Heaven.

7. FACING THE MUSIC

It's really tough having a lie-in down in our lane because the steep drive makes the milk float clank like mad. Also, my dad's latest thing had been locking doors but he was now also opening windows. Whatever! Apparently, his sore bits from the fire woke him at night. This was making him go round opening upstairs windows, to let some airflow through. That's what worked before. Joan had offered him the use of her fan but that would be too easy. She did keep making us this soup to die for, so that was enough. Whoops! I mean nice soup. It was this chicken and veggies from her garden all mashed up, creamy, yum! I was practised at ignoring the milkman and random cars on their way to work but I was just too nosey when I recognised my dad's BMW, revving up. He had already been for his usual workout by now, surely, so where could he be off to?

I grabbed my mobile and pressed 'Dad' on my address book. He had a hands-free, so I knew he could answer. No answer, down to no signal. So I tried again. This time he answered, "Hello, John."

"Dad, are you late for the gym or what?" I asked.

"Or what? I've got the nurse looking at my burns. It shouldn't take long. I'd rather do anything else but... Think of what we can do later to take my mind off the stinging, it's bound to aggravate it again. We could go out for the rest of the day, think about it. Bring a mate, if you have to. Anyway, see you around noon." He sounded as if he was going.

"Yeah, in a bit. Be brave." I tried to show him I was bothered. Then I remembered what Mum would have done. So I thought I'd try it. I prayed. 'Lord, please be with my dad when it hurts. Amen.' And that got me to thinking; it was constant, that hurt was coming back. Well for me it was still lurking, this hurt. It was stopping me have any chance of peace, ready to bite. Like a Pit-Bull terrier or the devil. So I reckoned that for Dad, it would be the same.

I had to make the effort to get dressed, just in case I might take delivery of another food parcel. Someone had to do it! Whether it was because we were men and incapable of doing for ourselves or just that people didn't know what else they could do for us, it didn't matter. It was great getting regular cakes and goodies come freshly made. Mum would have been pleased that her friends were helping, from all directions. Not like our relatives, who promised things you know they couldn't deliver. Work gets in their way, I know. But still, I felt sorry for my dad. His friends were useless at being there for him. Like I was useless at getting myself together, too many games and messages! And I would have to chuck Jez out who was still cocooned in a sleeping bag on my floor, rotting. I tempted him out with toast, that usually did the trick.

Eventually, I dived in the bathroom with this idea of going out for the day and who could come with us, going around my head. I mean. It's a bit sad when it's just you and your dad. Then I thought about it, if he's sore he might not be that good company. No, I'd leave asking anyone to come with, avoiding the friction. So smelling like I was out of a 'Lynx' ad, with my hair standing up all over, I went to the door when the bell rang expecting Joan with her lunchtime effort. My face must have coloured up. It was only, Hannah. She looked fantastic filling the doorway with all things delectable. Not just the apple pie!

Instead of taking it off her and saying thank you, I was there fumbling about checking out my flies were done up. I noticed that my jeans, down to dad's Navy ironing now had a stupid line up the front of each leg. I tried to rub them out. What an impression, couldn't fail! Der!

Luckily for me, she brought her sense of humour with her. "Don't worry about me!" she said. "I mean, I've got all day to stand here holding this thing. The pie survived my cooking but don't push it, if you leave me here much longer it might internally combust! That could be a good thing, anyway."

"You're joking, no way! It smells delicious. Sorry, this is me, just woken up," I said, lightening her load.

"Well, can I come in or what?" she went on. I totally forgot to ask her taking the pie into the kitchen. Getting my priorities right.

"Yeah, what have you been up to?" I asked, showing some interest. "How did your results go?"

"Well, I got to Fuengirola, in Spain for my jollies. Amy came with us, it was absolutely boiling. And exams err, not too bad. They let me back for sixth form so, that's good enough." She backed off a bit, covering the pie with a tea towel. I knew she wanted to ask how

I was but instead she said, "Youth club's back on after the holidays, you ought to come down. Paul could do with a few of your wacky ideas, to stop him getting boring."

"Yeah, definitely. It would help if I knew what day it was but I will do that. I'll come down, join the crowd soon," I told her.

"Shall I text you then, next Friday, so you know it's on?" she asked, then, "I could find out what we're doing to see if you fancy it. Only, if you like."

Before I could answer, the phone went. Hannah started towards the front door as I said, "Okay, thanks. See you later." She let herself out as I lifted the receiver a little hesitant, "Hello."

The reply came from a familiar voice, "Is that you, John?"

"It is," I replied, "that's Janet isn't it?" I recognised her voice from visiting Mum at the hospice. She seemed okay, then. Not too pushy. She let me make my own mind up about how Mum was looked after there. They were kind but somehow didn't pity Mum, which was important. There were these nurses that took her pain away, even better. They had these magical therapy rooms that relaxed you, with weird music going. Mum loved going in them. For some reason I liked the cook, too. Janet started talking but I dreaded what she wanted. My mind wasn't on her but I had an awful idea. Did she want to give us some counselling?

Then she was asking me, "How are you doing?" A difficult one!

As usual, I gave the robotic response, "Yeah, fine thanks." Why she asked when she knew I'd lie, beats me.

She came back with, "Well, it's just I've got some good news for you both. Can you let your dad know that your mum's self-help booklet has made the publishers? And they've agreed to go ahead to put the booklet in print. It will take a while but by the end of the year we should have a mock-up. She deserved to be heard, your mum."

It took me a while to get my head round what she'd said. Then, it was something else I had not a clue about. Typical! Then, I thought, "Go Mum!" and I asked, "what's it called, again?"

"Oh, of course, it's called, Letting Go," she said.

My voice went wobbly I managed to reply, "Great, that's really great." I needed to read it! Why hadn't she run this by us before? What did Janet mean about her being heard? Bizarre. It was as if these women talked a different language to me. Did she think Dad and I didn't love our mum? That was well out of order! I was in deep thought when she coughed. So I replied, "Okay, I'll let Dad know when he gets in. Thanks."

"Thank you, John." Not giving up she went on, "I think, the best quote from the booklet is, in all things God works for the good of those who love Him. Which is just your mum! Don't you think? Trusting God. You do know that she loved Jesus with all her heart, don't you?"

She waited, acknowledging my, "Okay." I knew but that didn't mean I understood. I was a bit jealous that Mum had thought of others in making a booklet, when I just got a letter. A letter about me being a 'proper son.' Yeah, right.

"How could she leave me out?" Slipped out loud from my big gob.

So Janet went all apologetic on me and finished with, "Well, the strength to face death and look forward to eternity in heaven, is what Jesus gave her. She wrote it for everyone, including you." She sounded like she knew, "Don't forget where we are if you need us. Bye for now."

"Okay. Bye then," I let the receiver crash down. All churned up, I was thinking that could have been done better. I could hear my mum say, 'We aren't meant to know everything and it's for God to sort out.' Shocked, I felt I'd gone back to square one. I mustn't hate people when it's not their fault. So much for having the time to think about anything else! That's when I had the idea that we could visit Mum's grave today and take some flowers. Perfect timing, a text from Athena, 'Slowly' was all she put. Ha! Easy? Not. I felt like texting back. But seeing that it was a response to my sad and lonely stuff, the night before, I let her off. Her knowing I wasn't that good at slow, me wanting to fix things, now. She was a best buddy. I let her in on it. She liked the buddy bit but not the way I text her, 'bbwb' the with boobs part she didn't appreciate it. Some Greek thing, maybe?

I let Dad put the kettle on before I told him about the phone call from Janet. Cutting him a slice of apple pie giving off eat me waves, I said, "And that's from Hannah. You know, she even provided the squirty cream. It's bound to make your sore bits better!"

"Oh, yeah! She sounds a bit of all right. So, your mum is going to be published, eh? Excellent! Did Janet give you a hard time?"

"Err, Dad, she wants to help, that's all." I was giving her a break. "Anyway, she wants you to give her a ring about something." I shrugged avoiding more problems. "And Mum, she's done real good, you're right."

My dad rubbed his new bandage, throwing some painkillers down his neck. "So, my idea about going out, is it going to happen?" He asked, all moody.

"Of course, I've got a great idea for that one but it can happen later. Ring Janet first, I thought you had some paperwork you wanted help with," I said, ignoring his mood, wanting him to get off my back.

"I got the blue suits to help with that one but I suppose you're right, at least the hospice knew your mum and that she wasn't just an average Navy wife." He looked thoughtful and picked up the phone so I left him to it. I needed to get outside and practise some kick flips. This was all getting a bit heavy for me. It wasn't my agro. Trying to ear-wig his phone conversation on my way out, I was listening for the lie, when asked how he was. 'Fine, thank-you.' Or would he start to be real? I missed it.

8. LETTING GO

When he came out to join me with another mug of tea, he seemed less wound up, saying, "I'm pleased for your mum, we should let people know. It's just a pity…"he started.

"I know," I interrupted, "and I'd rather she hadn't needed to write it at all! Will it make much money, did Janet say?"

"Well, if it makes anything you can decide what we do with the money, to remember your mum by. If you want?" he surprised me. "Otherwise we could give it to the British Legion."

"No cos then that would be your thing, not Mum's. You scank!" I could do that. I could sort something. "Cool, consider it done," I told him. One thing at a time went through my head. "Did Janet say we could go in?" I needed to know.

"She did actually; we could go to make a memory box up of our Annie. I thought that was a good idea and we might be able to clear some of her things, in there. I'm not sure how big this box is but what we've got to think about is whether we do it just us two or in a group?"

"No way! Surely, most of them are mourning old people, just remembering their like, grandparents or something. That no way counts, like your mum," I spurted out.

"Another time, later. Yes, I'd rather do it with just us two, but I thought I'd ask. Janet says sometimes it can work better." He paused and rubbing his tash continued, "She said something else. It made me proud of your mum. She said that with the booklet being published, that your mum left a legacy."

"Really? What's one of them then?" I wondered.

"It means something to remember her by and keep up with the good work, kind of thing. So we must try to plan a suitable memorial and a trust or grant? What do you think?" He asked.

"Yeah, whatever! Sounds good to me. How much are these guides selling for - £5.00 or more?"

"You know your mum, she didn't want anyone to miss out so they're going to be given away with donations if the buyer wishes to," he said with his eyes wide.

"Typical! We best not expect a fortune, eh. We'll carry on her good work but it won't have to cost much." Then I felt a bit down, knowing how tight the locals could be around here. 'The church might cough up?' was going through my head.

Sensing all this, he went on, "Just think of all the people your mum might help, though. It's absolutely brilliant! I'm going to get onto Janet and see if we can hurry up the printers, there're people with terminal illnesses that need to read it now, not next year. That might be too late." He was quite fired up. With his mission in hand he lifted the receiver. It was good to see that even at his age he could still get worked up.

I thought about the apple pie again but my mobile was sending off a message-received tone. So I flew up the stairs to enter the chill of my nicely, messed-up room. It was from Hannah, to remind me Friday was tomorrow. Ha, ha very funny. I texted back saying her pie had set my stomach off and that I was stuck on the loo, just to wind her up. It worked. She told me there wouldn't be any more pies, then. That backfired! But I wound her up with a bye text, 'aatf.' It meant, always and totally forever. Making her scared.

I put my earphones in and tried to just, be. For some reason, on hearing Hannah was back at school, my head was full of going back to do my retakes. I had totally messed up my GCSE's; Mum being ill coincided with just before the traumatic time. So I wasn't my brainiest, then! I had passed resistant materials, I.T. and I got an 'ology' (always handy!) but just missed out on the most important ones. My excuse wouldn't last much longer and secretly I was missing the whole studying, day to day.

I could go back in the New Year. Would it be better going to college to do the retakes, so no one knew my sad story with a new beginning or should I milk it for all it's worth at sixth form? Umm. These were difficult decisions, all too much for my micro brain to think about now. Ideally, all I wanted was to go back to last year's classes and do a complete rewind. That would be ace, rewind and do everything properly. Not chase girls and do tricks on skateboards but talk to my mum, whilst I could. I'd been a prize twit. Why didn't I just say, 'Me too!' once in a while after the dozens of times she told me she loved me? I pulled my duvet over my head to pretend it wasn't happening. Please, God. Make the clocks go back like in 'Back to the Future' and change history. I might even get a little brother then. That's what I wanted for years. That was maybe pushing it. Mum would be still be here with us though and I wouldn't feel crap all the time.

Dad interrupted my feeling sorry for myself session, banging on my door shouting. "Come on down when you're ready for some lunch, it's on the table. And I've some good news." Only lunchtime, I didn't care. And another roller coaster of feelings, I don't know if I had the energy left…

After a quick sausage sarnie, he was blabbering on about a memorial something. I couldn't do interested, so I took some orange roses from the vase, where Joan had recently plonked them and headed down to Mum's grave. Dad actually caught up with me despite messing about with pulling on a coat. There was a headstone now and the mound was flatter. It was absolutely freezing there. Eek! But it had a lovely black slate with 'In Loving Memory of Annie Jane White, 7.8.1959- 21.7.2008' on it, in gold. Classic!

Dad said, "The hospice have helped your Mum arrange all this, it's great isn't it?" I nodded. She was starting to blend in, like the poor old others. I was amazed at how many flowers, chrysanthemums I think, there were already on her grave. Not all from my dad either.

"Look at all these," I said. I read a label from the W.I., attached to a pink arrangement.

Dad wasn't fazed saying, "That's nice. It shows how much they appreciated what your mum did for them. All that 'popping in' paid off!" I thought it was funny that Mum had never gone for a proper job but then how could she, when Dad had been on duty so much? So she volunteered and did churchy stuff. We chucked the old limp, dried up flowers away. Then I read the stone. There was the usual bit about, 'Beloved wife of Steven and mother of John,' which made me feel sad and then some more, 'Seen the light, safe in God's Hands.' Right at the bottom was an old fashioned bit, 'In Heavenly Love Abiding.' Huh! What was that all about? I needed my mum to live here with me, some more! I had to admit that, with all the flowers it looked an okay place to be, if you had to be dead! I turned away. I wanted to run. How could she be happy to let go? I needed to get somewhere more upbeat. Where it was happening. I just left Dad and escaped.

I legged it, again. All of a sudden I went back to being this small boy.

Small.

Cold.

Alone.

But, away from the awful truth. This time, I was tucked behind the youth shelter. I was just starting to shiver these huge rattling shivers, when my dad found me. My guts had gone cold. I began to shout, "Bog off!" thinking it was my mate, Jez. When he got me he gave me this look, like I was loopy. Then Dad just slid down the wall of the back of the shelter next to me. Random! There was this foul smell of sick in the shelter, that's why I'd gone round the back. But it was rank there, as well. A stale smell of weed lingered. Mum used to say it smelt like rats! I was looking for an empty place when my head was full. My mind had gone into overdrive, considering the BIG picture. I wanted the world to stop spinning, to realise that things weren't right. But it kept on going. Dad looked completely freaked. And I thought I might be in for trouble. Then he went and put his arm around me.

"You need to get out of this hole!" he said, pulling at my hoodie. Now he was pointing, "Mind yourself on that sharp. I didn't realise that they took hardcore drugs down here." Amongst an old firework and some nub ends, I was shocked to see the needle. "Why come here, son?" Only, this time he was accusing.

"Look Dad, I didn't think about it much, it just happened. You know? Stop reading things in and no, I'm not doing drugs. I'm not totally screwed up!" Putting him right.

"Point taken, son. Come on then, let's go home," he gave me no other choice, tightening his grip over my shoulder. It felt good. I was losing a fight that I didn't particularly want to be in. It was nice letting him be the grown up, for a change. My sigh might have let him know that. We took ages to get back. The promise of a cuppa with dunked chocolate hobnobs, got us there. When I got in, the warmth hit me so I kicked off my manky Nikes and flopped on the sofa. Message received tone on my phone. Ben again, probably.

After checking Ben's message out, "Dad!" I shouted through to the kitchen.

"Yes, kettles on, it won't be long," he was whistling away.

"Ben and everyone are camping out tonight. You'll be alright if I go won't you?" I thought if you don't ask you don't get! I wished I'd not bothered, it changed things. Mr. Super Serious put his health and safety hat on.

He came back with, "Hold on a minute. I mean does everyone include that Joe? Where are they camping out exactly and do you realise it's close to freezing out there? You're not still in Greece you know!"

"Yeah, I wish! Isn't that more reason to camp, before the weather gets too bad? Go on, Dad. Hello, I haven't seen Joe in ages. You know you want to say yes." I was pushing it now.

"And still, where? Why?" He asked too many questions. Not worth it. I couldn't convince myself, never mind him.

I told him, "For a laugh, that's all. It'll be a good laugh. By the canal with me mates."

"And how do you think you'll keep warm down there? It's a SSSI, with scientific interest, that certainly means no camp fires."

This bitch of a response from him, was not helping, "We'll have a small fire then. Guess what? No one will ever know. We'll hardly burn the place down with all that water. Come on Dad give us a break. In your day, you used to jump off the bridge into the mud! Remember? I tell you what, I won't bother going in the water, if that makes you feel any better!" Me being a bit sarcastic now.

"What would your mum have said?" Came out his mouth with this daft look. "Why don't you have someone stay here, instead?"

I took off. He was classic. "I don't believe it! What's your problem?" I howled, trying to blink the past year out of existence.

"My problem? My problem is your lip, young man," he shouted back.

"Arrh, forget it! I'll not bother having a life!" I went stomping up stairs to crash. I was feeling angry and I needed a sadectomy. Or was that my Dad who needed one? So I turned my headphones to blast and shut it all out. I must have gone to sleep soon after, not remembering anything else. I can't have been that fussed about a camp. Would have been nice to have the option.

And it was Christmas, me unwrapping Pokémon cards and a Nintendo Wii. Mum got a new brown handbag and these posh silver slippers. I was playing tennis verses my dad when Mum brought in this delicious chocolate log...

Then I woke up sweating. Pity it wasn't real, just a dream. Worse luck. Nothing much was happening. I couldn't be asked to do anything. Apart from emailing Athena, that is. She told me Demetrius and Dad had been chatting, too. For some reason, I felt a bit of a cheat. With my dad, I made sure I kept my head down all afternoon.

So, by the time youth club came I scootered via the shop, getting my usual. With some questions for Paul, that weren't for Dad's ears, I hung around. I was really cross with God. He'd taken my mum when I still needed her. The cheek. That's what I'd tell him. There were all those murderers, rapists and cheats and still God took my mum. He picks the sweetest flowers first. That's what it said in the graveyard, on a kid's gravestone. What a load of crap! I took my letter from Mum so he could explain it to me, properly. He was probably sick of seeing these letters. Tough! He'd soon rush home to his sweet young wife and play happy families.

When I got there I made sure I was a bit early and went straight into his office. He looked spaced out and checked his watch. As I handed the letter to him I asked, "I mean, I do know it's supposed to make me feel better but what am I to get from it?" Before I could finish he was reading it out loud. I wasn't expecting that. He was smiling, smoothing the crumpled paper over his opened bible. He may as well not have bothered, because that's where the words first came from. He even read the 'love you' bit. Just him reading it made it a bit more official. He said it went,

> *'Like a sheep he was led to the slaughter,*
> *And like a lamb before it's sheerer is silent,*
> *So he opens not his mouth.*
> *In his humiliation justice was denied him.*
> *Who can describe his generation?*
> *For his life is taken away from the earth.'*

"Wonderful isn't it?" Like, he was asking me?

"Is it? Well, I know she's talking about Jesus but what's that got to do with her?"

Paul got all excited, "What I think she's saying is that Jesus died on the cross for her, so she didn't need to worry. The reason why is in this next part because deep down she believed this for her future." I saw that his eyes were all watery for this bit:

> *'And I will show wonders in the heavens above,*

And signs on the earth below,
.. before the day of the Lord comes,
the great and magnificent day.
And it shall come to pass that everyone
who call upon the name of the Lord shall be saved.'

I knew what it said; I could read! He was aggravating me now, I wanted to get it. Smiling, he leant back in his chair. While he had a moment, all I could picture was my primary school nativity play. It was the language, like 'and it came to pass,' which meant now't to me. All I remember was feeling ripped off being a shepherd, when I wanted to be Joseph, him being in charge of a donkey not some daft sheep. Still, I was missing the point. It must have been down to the minging stuff that was clogging up my brain cells.

"She called on God so she'd been saved. Right!" Sorted! I'd got it. She's safe in heaven. Great. I smiled back at him. Then I burst into the youth club hall and nicked the pool cue. Now it was my turn. Ben took me on. Wrong move. I won. Ben would never let me win. He wanted a decider game or two, no chance! I couldn't face losing. So I left.

My mates must have thought I was well out of order. I wasn't exactly using them but it was just I had so much going on that I forgot about their crap. And I forgot to say 'bye' and 'I'm doing okay' and then wondered why I got all these texts asking, 'what's up?' Riding my scooter flat-out helped. Then I went through the kind of letter I wanted my mum to write. Line by line I reinvented it. Closing my eyes it was there on a page. So that I could get it, not so dramatic like:

To John,

Forgive me, my time is running out. I thought that there would be more for me. My body is like a sand timer with the sand of life, slipping through at an alarming rate. You'll get that as you get older. It's completely out of my control. Just make sure you know I wanted to say something earlier but you were having fun. I couldn't do it. I wanted to keep you smiling. I never meant to disappoint you. My story is a success story and I don't consider I've lost anything. So neither should you.

Sorry, I couldn't say the words to your fresh face or risk more sadness, so here I am trying to write the words down. I hope this is okay. Firstly, I love you. You were planned and longed for and I will miss you. I'm sure your dad will do his best. You've got to stick together, you two. Will you do that for me, son? Please, look after your dad. He can be difficult to get near but that's what his job's done to him. He wants to be a good dad to you and he will be. If only you let him.

I hope that you two will kick back and really get to know each other. You have so much to give one another. If I've held onto you to protect you, it's been because I love you. Let Dad have the chance to do a better job than me, please. Try not to worry about me. I'll be safe with your Gran. The bible promises me that in heaven,

'God will wipe away every tear from our eyes; there shall be no more death, nor sorrow, nor crying. There shall be no more pain, for the former things

have passed away.'

That's good enough and I believe it. I hope you and your dad can understand and have peace about me leaving. Goodbye, my darling son,

Love Mum   x x x x x x x x x x

Better. I stopped and fell in a heap. No way could I have done that. It was Mum telling me, in words I clicked with. I know. She was there in my head and that was fine. I just sat with her a while, soaking her words in. Awesome!

9. TAKING BACK CONTROL

I wasn't that tired when I got back from youth club. I thought about the thrashing I had given Ben on the pool table before. The best! The punch bag looked pretty good for getting rid of some more energy. An hour went by, no problem, in the garage. Creeping upstairs I didn't bother messing about in the bathroom. Putting my ear to his door, I couldn't hear any talking to his friend. Just snoring. So I'd leave it all till tomorrow. My pillow did well as a flannel and then I flopped.

I'd even missed loads of texts from my mates. When I came round, it was well quiet in our house. Scary! Then I remembered, this morning Dad was starting his counselling, at the hospice, at last. We'd all been on his case about getting some help. I was fed up of him pacing the landing at night. Our annoying floorboards gave him away. Well, either that or we had these huge mice! Because my dad wasn't sleeping he was getting more wound up. That made him bad tempered.

So when he eventually poked his head in, I asked him, "What did they say?" I wanted him to be sorted, like I was. All I knew about the hospice was they did wicked cakes and big hugs. He explained his sleep deprivation was down to all the agro he was getting from the Forces, putting on the pressure for him to return to work. He wasn't up to it yet. Even I knew that. He hadn't got his head back together. Returning to the hospice was bad enough, "I had to walk round the block before going in," he told me, as the last time he was there it was heavy. He told me that the Navy made out as if Mum was all finished and forgotten. He had to stand his ground; at the hospice they agreed. I really rated him for that.

He told me he'd talked about going over Mum's letter time and again and how he'd got stuck. These letters of Mum's were proving to be high impact. They got us questioning and talking. How clever was that? What he couldn't get his head round was the bit where she put, 'I know I'm healed.' That was a hard one, as she did actually go and die on him! Then, Janet from the hospice explained that there wasn't a cure for her cancer. Not this secondary sod. She thought that what Annie had meant was, she'd come to terms with her illness and knew that her life was to end. This was because she looked to God. My eyes felt like they were about to pop out my head, down to my dad spouting all this off. He was describing how she'd put it to him. It was great he had taken in so much.

He said, "Jesus is like the bridge to God, heaven and eternal life. Janet told me. So that's why Annie didn't worry for herself. It didn't mean she didn't care about leaving us, either. It's just she was trusting God to look after us." He smiled. Janet had helped him get his head around Mum's happiness in her last days, despite all the agro. He had put it down to the morphine before but now he knew. He went on telling me, "Thinking about it, I'm afraid I've got absolutely no chance of joining your mum in heaven. You might stand a chance though, son." He laughed, a bit nervously.

I pulled him up, "Why do you think that Dad?

"Well, it's obvious. You have a clean slate to start with. Stay clear of trouble and you'll get ..."

I interrupted him, "No, I mean, what makes you think YOU can't get to heaven?

"Oh, well. In the name of fighting for my country I've done all the sin stuff. No chance! Stands to reason. You know, I've shot too many torpedoes, to land myself a place in heaven!" For now, I had to be happy that he was sure my mum was in a safe place. He still thought he was beyond God's love and forgiveness. Shame.

"Next time you go, can I come with you?" I asked.

"Yeah, of course. Why?" He looked through me.

"I thought of something I'd like to ask Janet myself. About lymph glands, if you must know!" I was thinking inherited stuff as well, but I wasn't telling him that.

He nodded and looked away. I wasn't going to feel guilty for being honest because there were things I was wondering about too. Like whether the docs did all they could do to stop the cancer. I know they tested her, took cell samples from under her arms. Why hadn't they picked up on the cancer spreading then? I had these things whizzing around my head that needed stopping.

But another time because we had to stop ourselves falling to bits without the glue that held us together. Mum. She was our bond. Not much happened during the week. We just got on with it. Normal stuff. By Friday I was going crazy, it was all doing my head in. Time for a quick get away.

"I'm off down Melton. Catch you later." Was all I could think of to say.

"Need bus money?" he came back with - head down, still full of his own questions.

Although I said, "I'm fine," he shoved a fiver over the kitchen worktop to me as I went out. Wise decision, given my history! I'd done my share of walking back from town. And I just wasn't up for that.

It took ages for the 'Number 22' to come but luckily, there were a few of us stuck there waiting. The last bus had not shown up and some old woman my mum used to know went on and on about the crap service. I thought about getting a half fare but I bottled out at the last minute, as Jez had hassle from this driver before. We got weird looks, as usual, taking our scooters on the bus. I just looked them straight in the eye. Not bothered any more. I had got a right to be there, just as much as them. In town we hung around the college steps at first. I wanted to catch Hannah about youth club. Some stiff in a suit came out trying to move us on, giving us some rubbish about by-laws or something. He went on as if we had weapons of mass destruction when all we were doing was using his precious steps! I followed Jez at full throttle off to the park to get away. He was kicking beer cans off the ramp when I caught up.

"Where did you get to? I thought you were behind us."

"Only grabbing an eye full of Madeline Smith, that's all!" I laughed.

He gave me a long look saying, "Oh, yeah in your dreams

and I saw Timberland shopping at the pork pie shop! Whatever!"

But it was kind of true. This immense girl, called Maddy, had actually flagged me down. I couldn't pass on that! We caught up with the latest. I don't know whether the kiss'n'tell, was in sympathy, or what. But I didn't care. I liked it. Who wouldn't?

We had a good session on the half pipe, before this townie gang turned up. Best time to go for chips. It was getting dark and freezing. As we scootered past the park we saw the same lot were still there so decided to head back home. It was a good move. Hannah was in the bus queue. When it came I let Jez doss down across the back of the bus by squeezing up close to Han. She filled me in on a few things. Her smell was intoxicating. As I tried to impress her it dawned on me that I didn't smell quite so good.

"Later," is all I said. So I just went back to slide next to Jez. He ponged worse than me. The bus was warm and the rocking made my eyes shut. There was this bad lad offering happy sweets round, for a price. It was that Joe again. Not the old Joe but one I hardly recognised, looking so ill. The stench of pot was familiar on him. We passed on that, too.

So he went onto this seat full of gals that told him, "Get lost!" He wasn't exactly a good advert for his gear, looking so messed up. My knees ached like mad; it was quite nice to chill. When we arrived in the village Jez wanted to come back but I knew I just wanted to grab some nosh and a blasting shower. He wasn't very happy but tough. He had stayed already this week. He was hungry and stinking but we let him crash on my floor. Normal. His feet were so bad! Instead of going home he headed off to the youth shelter to doss about. I told him, "See ya lata. Don't do anything wild."

Dad pointed to a pasty on the side that I grabbed on my way in. Two and a half minutes full power then a minute's wait. Bingo! Dinner was sorted. He wanted to talk while I devoured it. He was going on about hearing from Athena's family but I wasn't listening.

"Sorry, I'm off out again, in a bit," is all I could muster up. I needed to keep focused. It was my Friday night. The only time I ever went anywhere. It was a chance to get some more answers from Paul. They helped. He'd got pizzas cooking when I got there. Both Jez and Ben were in the house, keen to blag a free meal. Having made huge efforts, not! They hadn't even been home so looked well scruffy. Paul was tied up. His helper guy hadn't turned up or something. Why that pretty wife couldn't do it I don't know. Then there were some annoying kids who were asking for a clout around the ear. Not by Paul, he had patience. But one of them even had the cheek to come in smelling of ale. He was shown the door, totally knowing he had that one coming. The pool table got a bit of a hammering, something to do with the big freeze outdoors. I offered to help with the tuck shop just to try to get near Paul but that wasn't happening.

All Paul did the whole night was this talk about the message. He told us faith comes from hearing. Why not tell us something we don't know! Jez asked a good one. "So, you know the vicar's daughter? She thinks she's going to heaven cos of her dad but that's not it, is it?" He looked my way then went a bit red. So I smiled at him.

"No, not on its own but she may well have heard a lot of the word of God and acted upon it." Paul told us we all needed to get a personal relationship with Him. That Jesus was interested in all our stuff. Han kept me company for a while. She made it real easy to think about relationships. I thought she seemed to have a handle on life. It got a bit heavy when some of the young ones started being pathetic; so I decide to split, my idea being to avoid getting wound up!

Going out the door got Paul's attention, "What, you off already?" He said, noticing me.

"Yes, I've had it for today. I'll catch you later." I waved as I scootered off.

I heard him shouting after me from the back door of church, "See you around, John."

I suppose the answers to my questions were similar for the lot of us. That life wasn't a rehearsal. I remembered him telling us that one before. I just needed to doss. As I dumped my scooter I could hear Dad pounding our punch bag in the garage. "Night then, Dad, I'm back," I told him. Then I can't even remember hitting the sack.

I worked out the next day was the weekend because our house was busy again. Being the charity case of the minute what did we care? If it meant more pies I could string this thing out, no problem! I knew it was Joan who had been with the whiff of fresh buns, then the clattering got me wondering what she'd said to my dad. He was manic! Crashing about as though he'd lost something. A bit like when Mum came to the rescue, saving the house from being wrecked. And, of course it would take her two minutes to find his so-called lost shirt. She was great at tidying things away. It sounded as though he was knocking walls out and even I couldn't sleep through it. I poked my head into their bedroom. "Alright?" I asked the daft question.

"I will be, when I get this little lot off to the Cancer Research shop." He didn't stop to look up. Black sacks of differing shapes were being crammed, stuffed with clothes, shoes and all Mum's precious things. This wasn't right.

"Wow! Hang on a bit. Can't I have a look first before you chuck 'em?" I butted in.

"Whatever for? We're not going to get any more wear out of these, so somebody else might as well. They're right, out with the old."

"What do you mean? They're not just old stuff; they're bits of my mum! Well, her memory. To me, that is." I got up close pulling a bag right up and peering in. It was mostly her jumpers. They felt soft. Her perfume lingered on the top baby-blue one. I held it up to my face. "Do what you like, I'm having this one!"

"Okay," he said but he wasn't with it.

I was wrong. It wasn't Joan who'd set him off on a clear out but the Navy. Along with some Remembrance Day order of service details, they wrote to say they were after him getting 'ship-shape.' I saw it with my own eyes in this official letter on the dresser. We hadn't finished mourning Annie and they wanted him to think of his lost pals, as well! Why? He'd got enough crap at the moment. They could be cold-hearted swines. Where did his private life come into it? Or me?

When he said, "We've just got to move on," I knew they'd put him under pressure. He was robotic in his movements. Uh oh! I was worried about my dad. He wouldn't look at me. I pretended like it was normal, asking if he fancied a brew. He nodded, so I had my excuse to go downstairs and tip Paul off by phone that Dad had totally lost it. Well, I did try Sam first but he was out. As I went past the lounge I noticed that he'd even taken Mum's cards down, from the mantle-piece. To make way for the Christmas cards but even so. That worried me. But Paul was great saying, "I'm on my way. Just keep him busy there."

By the time the tea was brewed, Paul appeared at our back door. Dad didn't notice him come upstairs behind me, never mind suspect I'd rung him. Talk about a man with a mission but Paul was clever. He offered to help Dad get rid of mum's stuff. I'd never have thought of that one. Paul was good at convincing you that it was your idea to do something. I heard a question from him, "So you're dishing the lot, eh?" followed by, "There's no room to keep a few for John, just as a reminder of his mum?" No reaction at first. Then he went on. "Bring some tissue paper up with you if you've got some, John." There was just this continued, frenzied waste of energy. I couldn't watch. My dad had a definite problem. So I went to bring up the tea and get the tissue paper, wondering whether it was to get rid of me.

When I got back up Dad had a new pile of things he might like to keep after all. I plonked a packet of choccy biscuits on the bed for dunking, carefully picking out some beads from the pile. "That used to be your grandmother's. We can't let that necklace go. Those pearls are real, those. Not cultured rubbish or paste," Dad came out with.

"Can I have them, then?" I asked.

"Why not? But don't give them away or sell them, will you?" he came back.

"Bargain! You know, they're not all after pearls down the skate park, they don't go with hoodies!" With this paper I found at the back of a kitchen drawer Paul wrapped the pearls carefully for me, placing them in my hands. I offered Dad a biscuit. He shook his head. He'd got his precious letter from Mum when Paul sat down on the bed. Paul gave me a look, like he could deal with him.

"I've no idea what most of it means," Dad surprised us. "I've been over Annie's letter time and time again. What I can't understand is the bit where she says, "I know I'm healed." That's despite the fact that she knew she was about to die." He seemed confused by this, needing answers. Paul kept listening while drinking his tea. I made out I was studying the shiny pile of things.

Dad carried on, "Janet from the hospice explained to us that there's no cure for Annie's second cancer, the one that did it," letting out a sigh.

Paul picked up on this, saying, "What I think Annie meant was that she'd come to terms with her illness and was okay that her life here was ending. This was because she was looking to God for her future. And that she was trusting John's future with you, maybe?" My eyes must have gone wide. I couldn't believe he was letting Paul tell him this. Poor Paul, having to go through this again! Before, Dad would stop anyone talking about Jesus stuff. It had always been Annie's God, as far as my dad was concerned.

Dad was spouting all this off, describing how she'd put it to him. Janet apparently said, "Jesus was like the bridge to God, heaven and eternal life. So that's why Mum didn't worry. It didn't mean she didn't care about leaving us, either. She was trusting God to look after us for her." He smiled. I nodded. I tried to tell you, went through my mind but I was glad Janet had helped him get his head around Mum's happiness in her last days despite the pain. Before, Dad had put her bravery down to the morphine but now he knew. Great! We'd both got it; slow or what?

Then Dad went on to try to tell Paul the same spiel he'd given me, "I've shot too many of the enemy to land himself a place in heaven."

Paul wasn't having any of it, "Never! No one's done anything beyond the love of God. It's a free gift, this going to heaven, given by Jesus and not earned." He patted my dad on the back like he was a Labrador.

At last, it sounded as if Dad was convinced Annie was in heaven. There were these gruesome, deathbed conversion tales that followed from Paul. All along, I made out I was busy rooting through Mum's stuff. "Mustn't forget to go to the candle service, before Christmas. We should try to." Dad said, still rummaging. When I looked up his eyes were watery. I thought I'd leg it. Letting Paul deal with it, I heard Dad mutter, "I'm nothing without her. She's broken my heart and taken most of it with her!"

I was glad to be out of the way. On hitting my room, I dived in bed and pulled the duvet over my head. It's not my fault. I turned my ipod up and left them to it and had some peace for several tracks.

Paul gave me a shake to say he was leaving. Pulling my earphones out, I told him, "Thanks for coming round and I'll see you at youth club."

"He'll be all right you know, your dad." He tried to reassure me.

"Do you reckon?" I wasn't so sure.

"Yes, he's just at that stage, the one that you were at just after your Mum died." I must have looked blank because he carried on, "When I found you up there in those woods. Remember? You asked me to promise you that she wasn't really dead and that God would bring her back. You know, when I couldn't do that. You wanted someone to say it was some terrible mistake. And I've just told your dad the same. What you both needed to hear, that it's no one's fault and she's gone but safe. And certainly not forgotten."

"Arhh, good," I said, exhaling. "That's okay then. Cheers. See you later."

I thought he'd gone when he made me jump, coming back with. "Your dad has a lovely surprise in store for you at Christmas. That's a good sign, he's planning ahead," he was whispering. Then he left leaving me thinking. My brain hurt. Enough!

Han text a "ruok?" and I just wrote 'Book,' back. She knew it meant cool and she was on to me. But how could I begin to tell her the truth?

10. GETTING ON

When I heard the back door go I thought that Paul must have stopped chatting, a while longer. No such luck. It was the dreaded 'Little and Large,' otherwise known as Uncle and Aunt. I could hear her shrieking voice over my tunes. She was a right pain. Not what Dad needed tonight. There was a difference between helping and being nosey. She could wind me up at the best of times with her condescending tone. "How are you managing?" she would ask but didn't really want to know the answer. I felt for poor Uncle Sam, a real gentle giant. No kids, they might have made a mess and she liked things just so. By the time I got downstairs she was going off on one, on a hyper-tidy mode. How rude! She thought she could walk in and just start messing with our stuff. Crazy woman, Dad always said she was. He was talking to Sam eyeballing Aunty Pam, like he was about to fire, waiting for a clear shot. He was moustache twiddling, not a good thing! I knew the signs.

To save my dad getting into a state, I thought I'd wing it. I went straight up to my aunt; I wanted to ask what an earth she thought she was doing but instead gave her a hug. That threw her. Last time I'd done that I was about eight years old and left her hair coated in sticky chews. She looked a bit suspicious so I went along with it, saying, "Yeah, I'm much better now. The Greek stomach flu was a real pig to shift but I'm hardly ever sick now! Must have been part of the shock but then they weren't altogether convinced it wasn't contagious."

Bingo! You could see the cogs going round in her pea brain. "Really?" was her response, as she recoiled to the farthest side of the living room. Dad was so engrossed talking with Sam he didn't pick up on the joke.

I thought I'd push her buttons further, "Do you know Aunty, if you want to help out I think there are some sick-covered sheets still waiting to be washed in the utility. Only if you want to, and you're not worried about the chances of catching the awful bug yourself." She coughed and edged towards Sam. Pulling at his elbow, at about her height, she began whispering about making tracks soon. Sam looked a bit surprised, getting comfy catching up with my dad.

She justified her presence, "You know, John, just lately I've not been well myself. I need to take it steady. Need plenty of sleep to keep my strength up. Are you about ready, Sam? Let's leave these boys to get to bed shall we?"

Sam acknowledged her shriek and arranged to play a round of golf with my dad, before Christmas. I was doubtful that would come off but at least he was trying.

My Aunt nudged my Uncle towards the back door, very soon after that. Result! I laughed from relief that they'd actually gone, checking he'd locked the back door. But he looked drained, my dad. So, I thought about what Mum would do, when, "Do you fancy some supper?" came out my mouth. Dad had slumped into the chair and shut his eyes. "That's a no, then?" I thought.

I was just about to drag myself upstairs when he asked, "You can get me a glass of water, son? Please. I need to take these sleeping tablets with water."

I got on with it, passing him the glass. "Sorted. Night, then. I hope they work," I said, feeling for him. I rubbed his bald spot, passing by his chair. It dawned on me that I always slept. Dad was well out of his routine. More used to just chilling, me. It was starting to get to me, not doing much but I suppose Dad had a career waiting for him. He was probably fed up with home and just me. Boring. He would be better when he went back to work. I suppose I needed to think about what I was going to do but one day at a time seemed all I could do.

After my dad came up, I went to the notice board in my room for some bizarre reason. It must have been my sub-conscience talking because there it was marked in red, an orthodontist appointment on Thursday. This next week! A whole year ago my mum put a ring around the date, 14th December. As she did! Dad wouldn't even know I had a brace left on my bottom front teeth, you couldn't see it. But she knew, all right! She cared. And there I felt it again. Like, this heaviness. I was sad. Again. It wound me up! Surely, by now I should be getting over Mum? That's a question I should note down for Janet. Whether it was normal, all this sighing and feeling crap. I'd have to ask her. Settling down, it made me laugh that my dad had got sleeping tablets. What did I get? Sweet, nothing! Then again, I was just a kid. Right? I mustn't trouble my head with big questions. I could just hear my Aunt say that. Ha!

Then again, she did talk out of her backside!

As I came away from the calendar I thought how lame it was that I was getting excited about a dental appointment. Sad. There in the corner of my pin board I spotted the card Mum put up, with my name on. It was one of those things from the card shop with John on and its meaning-Gracious gift of God. Ha! That is what it said! She was soppy like that. It made me wonder what the name, Annie, meant. I'd see in the morning.

My text message rumble went off scooting my phone round in circles on my desk. I couldn't be bothered to look. I couldn't resist being sick of a completely boring existence. Maybe I just needed to get out more. It was Han who'd text me inviting me round. Dad wouldn't know if I sneaked out, he'd taken knockout pills. Tempting! Hanging out, that's all it was. Chilling on a Saturday night, normal stuff. Justifying having a life, I was. By the time I'd crept downstairs, pulling loads of layers on and managed to lock shut the backdoor; it must have been about half past twelve. The sky was magic with these piercing stars. I looked up and pictured Mum up there watching me. Reaching in my coat pocket, there was my beanie. Shooing off next-door's cat, I quickly pulled it over my tabs. And I scootered myself over to Han's sharp-ish, avoiding my extremities dropping off! Waiting, she opened the conservatory sliding door as I whizzed up.

"Long time," I laughed. "You not gonna be in bother over this, are you?"

"No probs," is what she came back with, letting me know

she had made me a hot chocolate by pointing to this table. "Help yourself," she said. It had marshmallows on too. Fantastic! It was sheer therapy. When I looked up she asked, "What's going on with your dad then?"

She caught me out, "What do you mean? How do you know?" I was curious.

"Too many vague questions from my mum, so I knew there must be something going on. You two have gone to the top of our prayer list, check if you like; it's stuck on our fridge."

"No, you're alright. I'll believe you. Wow, respect! Don't worry; it's just my dad's latest phase. He'll get over it, I Googled grief and it's all to do with Mum dying." I was whispering for some reason.

"What do you mean?" She went on.

She did ask and I knew she wouldn't blab, "Well, you know how I tell you when it's crap at home or I go off on one and you just put up with me?"

"Yeah, yeah, if you say so!" She gave me one of those giggles that made me know it was okay, so I carried on. "Well, my dad can't admit he's not got a handle on everything. He's going through this weird, tidy Mum away phase. I don't think he's eating much either. He's tried booze and now he's taking sleeping pills. He tells me to pull myself together but doesn't know how to do it himself."

"No! Really? " she said, seeming so much older than me.

"Yeah and what's even more weird is that he goes in these rages, where he's in his own world. Scary. I suppose it's to do with his other tough times, like in the Gulf. Then, the other day he actually said to me that I was lucky. Apparently, I'm lucky! That's because it was only my mum and he's lost his soul mate! "

"You are having a laugh? Poor you! He's in a sorry state, bless him!" Then she tucked in close, "I suppose I shouldn't tell you this but my mum reckons it could go back years, your dad, pushing things under the carpet. She thinks it could have built up from when your mum had that miscarriage, when our Sarah was being born. I can remember it, can't you? My dad taking us up the hospital to see my new baby sister and then us going in to see Annie with flowers and drawings? "

I gulped, nodding. Getting up from the cane sofa I paced around with these ideas pin-balling around my brain. "Han, your mum might be spot on. You don't think he feels guilty, do you? I know my mum was alone a lot, down to his precious Navy but..."

She blurted out, going red, "He's got unresolved issues, your dad. You shouldn't have to be helping him, all the time. Adults are pathetic. He could get loads of help if he wanted." She just looked at me and shook her head. "Sorry!"

"You're joking aren't you? Then he'd have to admit he had a problem and that just doesn't happen! It's like when Mum's cancer came back. He was supposed to tell me. Instead he avoided it doing everything for Mum and not letting me in on the big secret. The big chief got to do it all. I wondered why they had a big party. She was dying from a secondary lymph monster and all along I thought that she was getting better. She was saying goodbye to her friends but even then I didn't crack on."

I was agitated and Han was too. "You shouldn't have all this rubbish; I'm sorry to pass it on. He thinks by not telling me, it's helping. Do I look as though I'm still ten?" Trying not to raise my voice.

"No." She nudged up close when I flopped on the sofa. She was a good mate and knew far too much about me.

"I'm the first one to say we've got to move on but not by rubbing Mum out." I said to myself, mostly.

"It's a miracle that he's had his head together enough to think about Christmas." Looking away she realised she'd dropped herself in it.

Confused, I gave her a look as if to say tell me more, "Paul went on about something earlier, are you gonna spill the beans or do I have to tickle it out of you?"

"You'll find out sooner or later. You need something to look forward to. It's Athena. She's coming over to stay soon! And we're putting her up. It's about giving you a nice surprise. But now I've ruined it, soss!"

"Thanks for telling me; I can't take more secrets. Deal?"

"Deal." We sat there, smiling. But then panic came over me. "I'll have to get Athena something, a present. You know I've not got my head round the whole Christmas thing yet."

"Look, I've got a really lovely smellies set you can give her if you want. She's coming to see you, not for presents anyway." Han nagged.

"Ta, yeah. I'll take you up on that one, if that's all right. I know it's just..." I shrugged my shoulders feeling totally whacked. And getting up I said, "I'd better go. I'll catch you later."

"Okay?" She hugged me. Feeling better for the chat I needed my bed. The cold was getting to me but I'd let down some barriers and that felt okay. I crept in. It was now Sunday. That rang a bell. Dad would no doubt fill me in. I hope it didn't mean getting up at some stupid o'clock.

It was half past nine when Dad rushed in, bellowing, "We're due at church in half an hour, hurry up!"

Charming! Wonderful communication as usual, "Thanks for telling me. You go on your own, I'll make you late." I tried it on with him.

"I don't even know what it is we're doing." I asked as we rushed out the door to make our way to the church. It was only a short drive away.

My request to drive was just ignored. He huffed, "Didn't I tell you? It's called a candlelight service. It's to remember anyone you've lost; the hospice have arranged it for everyone down there." Eventually he got round to letting me know.

"Who's gonna be there, though?" I asked.

Again he didn't answer.

Luckily the church was heaving with people when we got there so we just mingled. I was fine until we sang one of the same songs as at my mum's funeral. Then it got scary. From then on I turned off. I let him go up and light a candle. Mum knew I loved and missed her down to the fact that I never stopped talking to her. It wasn't until we were filing out that Dad pushed me Janet's way, him saying thanks and embarrassing me big time with his nudging me routine.

"Oh, yeah, thanks." I didn't know what for. "And Dad said that I can come down some time, if that's okay with you?"

She attempted this hug thing that went a bit wrong but said, "Sure, if that's what you want. Fine, we'll look forward to seeing you same time next week then."

Great! I thought. Finally, I could get some answers and she might get Dad to face facts. To admit that he'd left me out the equation. Brave woman she would have to be to tackle me dad. Things had to change. He needed to let me in and let me have some responsibility for my own life. Mum surely taught him that one. Together, we could face the future. He needed to admit that he needed me as much as I needed him. He needed to be a man. Like I was. Mostly, with the exception when it came to the Orthodontist. That can well hurt. Luckily, it was okay that time, though. It was just a check-up, the morning after the candle service. My life was becoming so exciting. Not! I needed to get out more often. To do normal, whatever that was. To ever stand a chance of being happy again I needed to bring on the extreme or learn to live with it.

11. FACING IT

When I came back I re-read Mum's tatty letter, I felt I could do with meeting Janet, on my own. I'd got stuff that had to come out before I could share it with my dad. I knew Janet cared and she was far enough off for it to be just bearable - I might never see her again. Paul was great but he was somehow, too close. How could I begin to share my deep, scary bits with him? I needed him for the rest of my life - to rate me. But Janet I needed now, to make sure I wasn't going mad or worse, sad!

Dad had something on his mind. He'd been on one of those, self-help, bereavement websites. The paperwork was mounting. All I could hear was him making weird comments, "You know what they class me as don't you, on their silly forms?" He ranted.

"No," but I had a sneaking suspicion I soon would do.

"Well, I'm officially known as a SINGLE PARENT! Ridiculous!" You'd think that he'd been accused of a dreadful crime, or something.

I thought it was quite funny. "What's wrong with that then?" I smiled at him, "don't worry, you'd never be accused of being a chav!"

"For one thing I'm not after charity, if that's what they're trying to make out. I've never sponged off anyone and I don't intend to start now." He was whingeing whilst bashing away at the keyboard.

"As if," was all I could say, feeling quite a relief in giving Dad the slip, "I'll see you later then Dad, going out with the lads." I lied. I didn't want him to worry about me. He had enough on. And I didn't need him tagging along.

When I got there Janet was waiting around for me at the end of her busy day with the guests. The place was a bit spooky without the constant stream of helpful hands bearing tea and cakes. The easy chairs were empty but still tunes filled the lounge area with their vinyl versions of the latest hits. As she greeted me she made towards the music hub to switch it off, saying, "Let's not sit in here, John. There's a room that's better next to my office." I followed her.

I was surprised to see Paula, the secretary, was still giving her laptop some hammer at her desk. She glanced up, "Hello, John. Nice to see you again, how are you doing?"

"I'm good, thanks," responding politely but ignoring her because I wanted to just get this over with. Janet didn't quite shut the door but I knew I was safe. It was only Janet who could stand my worst nightmares. There was more anger to let out.

First, I rambled.

Then, I screamed and shouted. On this loud sofa were some cushions. Before long I was punching them. The 'it's not fair' moment reappeared that I hoped had gone. So it brought it all back. Back, like it was yesterday. Janet apologised, "I could have been more sympathetic with telling you about the booklet. I'm so sorry if I've ever over looked you, John. And your mum, well, she was in so much pain she had to think of herself. She was always my first priority but there is a child bereavement centre I can put you in touch with if you like? They're there to help."

I heard myself say, "Oh, that's okay." Only then, then, I cried. Paula bought in some water. We already had tissues. Then, I saw Janet was crying, too. Useful? Yeah, in a way then I didn't feel on my own. And we all have our own problems.

She tried to tell me it was all, okay. And she said, "We all do it differently - getting used to someone leaving us. We never forget but we adjust."

Nodding, I got it now. I had to adjust to not having a mum. Instead, I'd been left with this empty space. But I could learn to fill that with nice memories of Mum. Like her stew and dumplings or her wacky songs…Janet explained the first bit after Mum's death as the worst ever.

Like,

TOTAL CONFUSION…

"You're telling me!" I agreed. She made me realise that Dad had somehow wanted to blank this bit out to protect me. So that's why he took us away to Greece but in the end all he'd done was, delay our sadness coming out. On the wall she showed me this poster called, 'The Spiral of Grief'. It was a lot like what Paul was going on about. I didn't want to look at it but she assured me it could give me some answers. With a black hole in the centre that related to the time of Mum's death, all around were these feelings I saw that had been eating away at me. Complicated stuff like denial, sadness, anxiety, pining, anger, shock happiness and relief. On reading them, flashes of times when those feelings crushed me came in my head- some straight away, some later on. So it came as a relief, that I was being normal. And I told her, "Yeah, done that, been there. I don't know about the relief until now but I've definitely had the happiness bit and then felt guilty after. So I think I should get the T-shirt!"

"Sorry. No T-shirts but I've got some great wristbands, if you want one? It's to remind you of Annie. But you need to take the message for yourself, too." She gave me this weird smile.

"That sounds good to me." I said, nervously.

"Here." She reached into a drawer bringing out a blue woven band. It had '*Loved today, yesterday and forever more*' on it.

"Wow, thanks," I said, letting her tie it round my left wrist.

She told me it was all healthy, what I was going through. The pain had come out in a controlled way, where people understood. She went on to say that I needed the security of a base from where to explore stories, to externalise my bad feelings. This was all a bit deep but when she told me about some group work with other youths in similar bother I was okay with the idea. It would be with this bereavement place where she got the memory box idea from.

"Yeah, go for it. I'll have some of that," I said.

So, she booked me a place at this outdoor centre, with the Youth Bereavement Centre in a month's time. That would be the New Year. She went on about being here for me and my Dad. That I'd taught her stuff! Enough already! My brain was aching. I had asked the questions about the details of Mum's death that I needed to. Janet was great telling me things honestly, like I was actually capable of taking it. Like my chances of getting cancer and that terrifying idea. Getting these facts I'd missed out on before, being overprotected, filled some of the black holes around Mum's death. And that somehow gave me permission to reflect on Mum's life. It made more sense, so I was a bit happier.

On leaving, she tried to convince me that the force of these panicky feelings should get less. I wish. She gave me a pamphlet called, 'Never the Same' about not accepting loss but learning to live with it. I liked the bit where some random kid like me said; "It's longer since my mum died so how can that be better?" Exactly! I read that bit in a speech bubble as I walked back to my scooter left against the fence. As I rode off pushing this pamphlet in my hoodie pocket, 'I hope I'll never forget my mum's lovely perfume' went through my brain. How bad would that be? The info looked all right, I'd read more later. For now I could keep going with what I knew. And I might just be able to help Dad a bit more. Though Janet did say I needed to think of myself first.

I called in by the skate park on my way home. But a whiff of bacon pulled me into the corner shop first, just as it was closing. I begged the last bacon buttie. Delicious! Ben moaned, "You jammy sod, they never give me owt!"

Scoffing the last bit, I gave him a, "bothered, am I?" before throwing myself off the half-pipe. After a full ten minutes of creating some seriously talented jumps, I stopped to get my breath back.

"Had a rough day?" asked Ben.

"What's it to you?" I eyeballed him knowing he gave a damn.

"Nothing! You're just blocking me, that's all. I wondered if you were after a fight!" He was just having a laugh.

"Well, I've found out I'm not mad - always a good thing!" As I finished talking Jez came up and barged in.

"You should be so lucky! At 6th Form today they were trying to say I'm mad, so I get help - more time for my exams or something? Bargain. All I need to do is keep on doing my funny thing and I'm A-okay, easy! Is that neat or what?" He was smiling, his crackers smile.

"If you say so, Jez, if you say so, mate." I laughed and Ben raised his eyebrows. It pulled me up, him talking about his day though because I couldn't get my head round my college course coming up in January. Too much! So I made some excuse up to get home. Jez was following me like he did but I told him, "Not today, Jez mate." I didn't know what to expect. You see, lately my dad had found the bottom of a whisky bottle, his absolute favourite thing. And I didn't want Jez part of that!

When I got home it was a relief. My dad wasn't even tipsy. He'd been in the loft and found the old tree. It was there in the lounge by the dining room. He was unwinding the fairy lights when I offered to help, after helping myself to the leftover pizza off the kitchen table. He asked me, "You don't know where your mum puts the Christmas decorations do you?" Looking quite put out, "I'd have thought they would be with the tree in a bin bag in the loft but I can't find them anywhere. She wouldn't have chucked those Victorian baubles she inherited from your Gran, I know."

"I'll go and have a look, shall I? The only other place I can think of is in the garage." I was thinking about an old dusty desk full of my old reports and embarrassing stuff I did way back in primary school. "She might have crammed the trimmings in the old desk."

Dad lifted his head up from his concentration as he checked the bulbs still lit, replacing the dodgy ones, "You've got a point there, nice one. Why she had to hoard everything I do not know!"

I decided to look in the garage first. I pushed the heavy punch bag to one side, so I didn't knock myself out but saw there was dried blood on it. Worrying! Dad must have given it a real whacking. I must give him a break. He was hurting, too! When I got round to looking, sure enough there were the tissue-boxed up best baubles and lengths of gold and silver tinsel. So I shouted through via the back door, "Found them!" Trying hard not to get side-tracked by the other precious junk Mum had stored there. That cheered me up a bit. I knew she kept lots of my school star work because she loved me. So I came through to the lounge with this daft, soft look on my face.

Dad said, "Go on then. Share the big joke."

"Oh, it's nothing. Just, I noticed all my first school stuff is still in there. That needs binning now." I put on my hard look.

Dad didn't jump to clear it away. "No, leave them there for

the time being. Paul says we shouldn't chuck too many memories away or we might regret it later."

Well impressed was I that my dad, having thought about it, had then gone on to outrank me on it. Like he cared or something. I should have hugged him. Of course, by the time we'd finished the tree looked like it had been dragged through a hedge backwards. But that was okay as it was a joint effort. All good. Leaning back to admire our handiwork he asked, "What are you up to tomorrow?"

Trying not to look obvious, I asked, "Why?"

It was then he just slipped into the conversation, "There's a special visitor coming to see you, that's all." He looked really excited and no way did I want to burst his bubble. He was definitely improving, getting his act together and I was pleased for him. So I made out like I was clueless about Athena coming and went on about Santa for a laugh. Then I felt a bit awkward and even a bit worried. Should I have emailed her more? I hoped she didn't think that we had used her family. I felt my cheeks burn. Dad saw I was miles away saying, "Wow, you really are worried about which list Santa's got you on, will it be the naughty or nice?" Then he roared with laughter. As he did.

"As if!" I gave back but it was nice to see him chillax, even when it was at my expense. Dad went to get a soft drink and watch the box whilst I decided a shower might be in order for my big day tomorrow. Because he thought he'd got me with the whole huge surprise thing. I let him get away with it. I remembered to wrap her present Hannah had got me, before I went to bed feeling a bit bad.

Everything made me feel guilty. I was a real selfish pig I don't know why these girls bothered with me. More effort required, then I got an idea. I'd Google 'Happy Christmas' in Greek and put it in a card, make out like I was about to post it. That should impress Athena and as for Hannah I think I needed to put some serious effort into thinking of a decent present, maybe take her somewhere. I could pull this off unless the girls talked. Then, I'd be stuffed!

When the morning started with my dad tidying up I would have been suspicious, that is if I'd not been tipped off already. It was Christmas. I had found out that Kala Hristougienna, meant Merry Christmas so wrote it in her card. I was thinking of an excuse why I hadn't posted it yet. I was brain dead when Dad went well into his role-play, barging-in making out we were off to see some long lost relative. When all along, I knew he was driving me to Hannah's. The story went that she was coming with us for some bizarre reason.

So I went along with him in the car to Han's, keeping quiet but thinking it fitted, grace. Grace, that's what the name Annie meant. She was full of giving me second chances and I know that must have taken some doing. For Dad, that worked as well. Even now, I could feel her love. The way she left things all sewn up for us. She'd loved people who now loved us, on her behalf. Well, tried to. As I walked in on a bit of a cloud I gave Hannah a wide-eyed look trying to be natural. It didn't hurt, using this grace stuff Mum had.

Then out burst Athena, obviously finding the whole secret thing was too excruciating. I hugged her lots, throwing in the odd,

"What?" and "I can't believe this!" for effect. Dad looked pleased with himself that he'd pulled it off. I gave Hannah a shove; she just smiled. Athena gave my dad a high five.

"How did you ever manage to get away from your family at Christmas?" I asked her. We were holding hands and spinning around the room at the time.

She nodded replying, "Oh, it's okay. You know, our Christmas, it goes on and on. We start on the 6th of December with the feast of Nikolaos; I've had most of my presents already! And we go on partying for a full month, finishing with Epiphany. And there's so much family that by the time they miss me I'll be back home. All that food! It won't hurt me to pass on the odd feast day. So with five days between flights, I'll cope." She giggled.

During this time of catching up Hannah and Dad had gone into the kitchen to make tea or something. And although I knew I couldn't keep this good thing going forever I took Athena in my arms and hugged her real tight. Her hugs were like the best ever medicine. I'd missed them. Then slowly I let her go. She didn't flinch or push me away. It's something she did a lot at home, naturally. It was a great early Christmas present to keep me going. She kept on, "The good thing is I can research possible Uni's whilst I'm here. You know one of my cousins is at Lincoln Uni? Why not? My dad will have it down as a business expense somehow. I know he will!"

"You're the best. I just hope it's worth you coming to boring old England." Thinking about it I added, "Round here there's only the skate park with it being freezing, you'll have to keep moving. You can borrow my skateboard if you like? And there's a corner shop but it's not as good as your cafe! I suppose I could take you to see Paul; he's carol singing around the village tomorrow night. After that if we get desperate there's a pool table down the pub."

"You do know how to spoil a girl, Johnny. That's where I come in young man," my dad chirped up. There's more to see of sunny England than just the Vale of Belvoir. We could take you up to our local castle but I'm actually treating you three to a night and a couple of days in London. You deserve it. We'll show Athena the sights and grab a show. What do you think?"

"Wow, Dad, are you for real? Yeah, I like that idea of us four heading off to the smoke. Sounds good to me, alright with you girls?" I was well happy.

We'd interrupted them, chatting as if they had known each other for years. At the same time they nodded, screaming crazily! There was all this long, dark Athena hair bouncing with Hannah's lovely, straight, blond bits. Mixed up with the loudest squeal. Then they got into close-up whisper mode, in between bursts of laughter.

"That's a yeah, then," I said to Dad who'd put them in touch via email apparently about a month ago. Like sisters, already! The next thing, out came a box of homemade cookies from Athena's magic bag. No surprises there, usual fantastic grub, Greek style. For Hannah there was this beautiful glass bauble for her tree. It was made by some clever Aunt, brilliant! Athena didn't get the whole 'wait until Christmas day' thing. Whatever! Before I could stop her we were being shown a press cutting from a Greek newspaper. Fantastic! There was Athena outside the café holding up a familiar Fanta bottle.

How embarrassing! I grabbed it off her asking, "What's it say?" then, hiding it when Ben and Jez poked their nose in. Luckily she left it as the boys arrived. I muttered under my breath, "I'll get you for this later." The lads were obviously keen to hear of two fit gals under one roof. Bargain! Never slow to find out about talent was our Ben! Dad backed off letting us chill a while and luckily missing the newspaper article. He had a grin the size of a football pitch on his face. It was great.

Hannah's mum was doing a fine job of keeping my dad busy but the thing was it was Christmas Eve. He pushed his head round the lounge door, "Don't think I'm a party pooper but if you want to catch the carols you'll need to head them off round at the church and you can walk back our way." Us lads did the required squirming as if singing carols was for wimps but quickly recovered at the first sign of enthusiasm from the girls. "See you back home then. Later," I shouted back to him. Coats on, taking in a long drag of icy air, we headed out the door to find Paul and his band of tuneful revellers. Five of us up the middle of the road, our arms tightly linked as if we owned the place, perfect! I thought then what Dad had done was just like something Mum would have done. The boy done good!

12. CHRISTMAS CAROLS

Paul was his usual welcoming self. He gave me a smile that showed me he was in on it. I heard Athena talking about Christmas services and where to go. I had to lend her my scarf. She already had Hannah's gloves on. "It never gets this cold back home," she said shivering.

"In a while you'll warm up. There's some warmed mulled wine when we get back; now that's worth singing for. They water it down or add orange juice or something," I joked with her. Hannah seemed to be getting on well and Ben and Jez who were there for the minced pies. For the carols she didn't know I suggested singing 'M & M,' explaining that this technique had worked for me, on the back row in church for years. It was really quite late by the time we had sung round the main lanes of the village. The version of 'Good King Wenceslas' Ben was singing, was a bit dodgy, but hey! Mostly the locals opened up the front doors to their centrally-heated homes to listen to us. Only those too tight to bother didn't, making me feel sad. Sad for them who had no reason to be hopeful at all.

Dad had hot chocolate and some pizza all ready for us at home, becoming quite the entertainer! I was well impressed. When he produced this small wrapped present for Athena I was even more shocked, in a good way. She looked a bit taken aback. "It'll help you two keep in touch," was what he said, giving it her.

"Thanks so much Mr. White. That'll help me keep an eye on

him," she said smiling, when she's ripped the paper off. He'd told me earlier he'd bought her something, online. I got close to Athena in the back of the car asking about the 'message in the bottle' affair. She told me not to worry and that she'd explain when we got a minute together. Fat chance I thought. After dropping the girls Dad was still so excited that he'd got her a webcam. He went on about it letting me actually see her face when I spoke to her on msn. As if I didn't know. But he'd got it right, again!

"Thanks Dad," is all I kept saying.

And he'd done extra good getting a Christmas day invite from Hannah's parents for us all to have lunch. Bargain. Athena expected to go to church Christmas morning since we'd missed her usual midnight mass on Christmas Eve. Paul let us know when the short service would be, 11 o'clock. We would have to unwrap our last few presents and pick them up for before 11. Slim chance!

Dad expected me to be ecstatic about having free driving lessons with him and some London show tickets, for my main things for Christmas. I realised it must be costing him a fortune, so I went along with it. "Just what I wanted, ta!" is what I said. Mum used to get me all the fun stuff. Crazy bits and bobs, like spud guns and she would have bought me some neat, scootering designer gear for sure. Ah, well.

"From now on we're going to do more fun things together! You and I." scarily he declared, meaning like going carting and stuff, I think.

"Great," I said and "can Ben tag along cos I owe him one?"

He looked all right with that. I felt a bit mean all I got him were some of his favourites - chocolate brazil nuts. He looked genuinely pleased. Still, he made me a bit sad. Our family had all gone mad on me and forgotten him. He'd just got vouchers, mostly. He hated shopping anyway, so vouchers were only bearable if he could use them to buy online. He'd manage that somehow. I'd help him browse. When our quick burst of unwrapping was over we trudged upstairs with our gear to get ready for going out. The house wasn't right, without the usual gorgeous cooking smells in like last year. The only things left under the tree were Ben's present and something for Jez. I'd catch them later. So I was quite pleased I had somewhere else to go.

"Come on then, Dad, more carols and minced pies. Church again. We're breaking all the records! It's not too bad really, nice to get out the house. Just beware of shaky Susan's hugs, cos you need escapology training to get out of them alive!" I told him. He looked worried having got out of doing services before, choosing to mind the turkey in previous years. That was when he was home, that is. This Christmas morning service was short but sweet and Athena seemed happy with it. She'd expected a full nativity scene but settled for the bible readings that mentioned Jesus.

When Dad asked her what she thought, she said, "Why is it mostly just the women not all the family, like in Greece?" He went a bit red at that one having not been there himself previously. But this year was different. He had done it, he'd come to church on Christmas Day and I was proud of my dad, tucked in his warm navy coat. Looking good. And he was less cynical. Paul was especially fussy and we had hugs from the pastor. I caught the sound of my dad saying he'd come back at New Year. Quite a big deal!

We were still humming, as we walked into Hannah's house. That gorgeous whiff was more like it. I wondered how early they must have been up to get everything cooked and come to church as well. Hannah's mum told me, "The answer is the Aga, it's brilliant! I put the turkey in last night; you'll taste the difference. The meat just falls off the bone but it's moist."

"I'm looking forward to it," I told her. The strong waft of turkey mixed with roast veggies hit us as we took our layers off in their hall. Their banister, full of coats was how homes should be at Christmas. Messy. Hannah and Athena busied themselves in the kitchen with my dad whilst I hid in the lounge. The movie channel was primed for a continuous showing, after lunch. Hannah's dad had that one sorted. By the time, "come and get it," was shouted, I was well hungry. I disappeared for a moment, out into their back garden. I hung around the bin to be alone. Just to breath. I said, 'Miss you Mum.' I said it out loud, so that she knew I hadn't forgotten her.

"Come on John, don't leave all the work to us girls," Athena shouted out the back door. Then, "You'll have to watch that, Hannah. He'll let you wait on him hand and foot." She laughed. Wiping away where my eye had leaked I went back in.

Dad glanced my way. The bubbly he had under his arm was uncorked and before we started he toasted, "Here's to absent friends, cheers!"

A quiet, "Cheers!" came back from everyone. Then Han's dad did a nice lunch blessing putting it into perspective. Then they all spoke about Christmas being a difficult time. My dad blew my mind saying about it, "Me being happy with one thing doesn't mean I'm not grieving about another."

The girls and me were even allowed one Alco pop each. As the glasses clinked I thought how Mum would have approved of us being with good friends at Christmas. We'd had random guests for Christmas meals before. It was different being on the receiving end. It felt right.

I never realised Hannah's parents were so great until today. The crackers were a novelty to Athena who looked quite shocked when the first one was pulled. After the gorgeous turkey with all the trimmings she seemed impressed with the lit pudding thing. "Just like a naming day back home, hey Athena?" I said.

She filled us in on her traditions, which went on for the whole month. Puzzled she asked, "Why do people rush back to the shops for sale bargains, on Boxing Day?" She'd noticed the T.V. ads. Dad shook his head, having no concept! Then again, we were going down to London but that was to show her the sights and do a few touristy things. So that was different. The show we were going to see was 'The Sound of Music,' a nice traditional Austrian story! We had a laugh at that.

The games after lunch included, Monopoly. This was useful for cluing Athena up on some of the names in London. Charades we decided would be too tricky. When the film came on Athena tried to look interested but soon got dragged upstairs to think about what clothes she needed for the trip tomorrow. Hannah was well excited making out she'd never been away before. I think it was because we had London Eye tickets and a boat trip booked, so it was going to be pretty full on. I wondered about the zoo but Dad thought that might be one thing too much to fit in.

So after a marathon telly watch that was Christmas Day, and some snoring from the adults we said our thanks and took the girls back home. This way we could get off at stupid o'clock in the morning. I was getting high from the girls' giggly, chatting. Dad found it less doable and chose to go to his room after seeing the girls into the spare room. My orders were to make them a hot chocolate, nightcap and then leave them to get a decent night sleep. We should have done that but it was half past one before we finished messing around watching random stuff and playing playstation games.

When Han dived in the loo Athena finally got to fill me in more about the newspaper thing. The reporter had been taken in by the whole sad story and actually coughed up the Euros for most of her trip. They thought I could do with a visit to cheer me up and she said they called me a 'holiday hero.' I felt myself go scarlet. She was grinning, telling me to keep the paper clipping.

I said, "Your family deserve it, you all work so hard. I'm glad they helped you with the trip." Giving her a peck on the cheek before letting her go up to join Hannah, who was getting ready for bed. I was still thinking how generous the Greeks were. Feeling I ought to get some sleep.

Next thing I knew Dad was whistling manically making embarrassing remarks about what not to forget to put in my rucksack. Morning already? He was giving up his footie for us; the Reds were playing at home. Wounded! We'd make sure to catch the highlights later on the TV. The girls had enough gear for a week but I suppose we were going out to the theatre which demanded some sparkly designer stuff. I had put in a grey shirt from Uncle Sam that I rated; with a pair of new jeans I was sorted.

The traffic wasn't too bad down to the end of the underground line where we were parking the car overnight. The train was exciting for Athena. She said, "There's nothing like this where I live!" She looked concerned when a woman with a baby was begging, handing out these cards with her details on. Dad had a word with the woman passing her something. He then joked that she had her Merc parked around the corner. I wasn't as good a judge of people as my dad but trusted him on this one. "What did you give her, Dad?" I asked.

"It was just some turkey and cranberry sauce sandwiches, kindly made for us," he replied, smiling.

Hannah went crimson saying, "Oh no! That's just like my mum, I'm so sorry. Did she insist you had them?"

"Pretty much!" He told her. We just sat there having a right laugh. As we got closer to London we pointed out buildings but then were in darkness. She thought it was funny losing her signal on her mobile. She was going to text back home as soon as she could to let them know what a great time she was having in the capital. We were heading for Russell Square.

Dad said, "You lot are high maintenance, this area is safe-ish but at least try to keep your money and mobiles out of sight. That's what I'm doing." We'd always stayed in the Docklands before but this was way closer to all the action.

As we came out of the underground the glistening lights of the shops and restaurants made the girls go, "Ahh!" There were these gospel singers collecting in the entrance who sounded really soulful. We could have stopped there.

I told Athena, "We ordered them especially for you!"

"Really?" She smiled, nudging Hannah. "Yeah, yeah!"

Dad and I just looked at each other and laughed. We wheeled the bags round the corner to the square that looked special this time of year too with twinkling lights in the trees. The staff on the hotel desk asked, "Can I have your passports, please?"

"Why?" answered Dad, handing her the booking details off the net. "We're from Leicestershire!" He gave a confident glance to Athena that told her not to worry. I thought how up he was.

"Sorry, it's my error. No problems, two twin rooms coming up, Sir." She remarked a bit flushed whist tapping into the computer.

Dad put her at ease saying, "We are a little early. We could leave our bags at reception if our rooms aren't ready; that will be fine."

She said that would help. The flu bug meant that they were short staffed. Keen to get out and about we dumped our luggage and went to find our bearings. Hannah had to explain loads as we moved like ants around the pavements with these skyscrapers either side when we got to the shopping part.

"Anyone hungry yet? I could have saved myself a fortune if I'd saved the sandwiches! I'm not talking to you John, you're always hungry."

"I'm fine, thanks," said Athena.

Hannah gave a cringe and said, "Me too, I'll kill my mum when I see her!"

Athena looked horrified. So Hannah reassured her saying, "Only joking!" We made our way towards the river and pointed out Big Ben. I took a photo and texted it to Ben. Ironic! He gave me some stick back about that. There were these tacky stalls selling statues of the Eye to which Hannah and Athena were drawn. Rip off! We got a can of pop and some chestnuts from a street-seller before we took our circular tour of London, on the wheel. Our pod was full of Chinese tourists, who were real annoying, flashing away on their expensive cameras. The Eye moved so slow giving Athena a chance to take pictures whilst we took in the view. Dad and me were waiting for the screams when we got to the top. The girls weren't too bad. Awesome!

Dad nudged me, whispering, "You know who would have liked this?"

I nodded. "That's just what I was thinking!" It was then I

realised that Dad was doing a good job of hanging out with us. He was an apprentice at this kind of stuff but he was doing it. After the snails tour the girls were keen to get a quick something to eat, leaving us time to get ready for the theatre. We wondered about a Chinese meal but because of time went for a Pizza Express. Now, Mum would have bought out vouchers for 3 for 2, or something equally bad. My dad knew how to party without scrimping. It was the first time I noticed something that my dad was better at than Mum. Bargain! And it felt okay. We needed to head back to the hotel to get ready.

Dad and I played on a pool table downstairs, so it can't have been that posh at our hotel. We had to, because we were dressed for the show hours before them. Boring! When they eventually turned up Hannah looked the best but I never let on. Dad said, "Johnny you look like a thorn between two roses, let me take your photo!" I couldn't believe him. Well embarrassing.

"Who's rattled your cage?" I joked, moving quickly out of his reach. Athena's eyes widened, like I'd done something terrible. The taxi ride to the theatre seemed a bit over the top but we'd have been late otherwise. The singing was all right but the dancing was a bit camp for me; the girls loved it. It was nice to be where it was happening. Dad had seemed a bit stressed at the rip off drinks prices so we had ice creams at the interval. We walked back finding it had been exhausting watching them on stage, never mind anything else. Back at the rooms I liked the huge bed I got best. I pressed all the buttons to find out what they did. I knew the girls would be finding all the freebies in the bathroom they might as well have ours, too. Dad and me had no use for them. Tomorrow was the boat ride.

Dad made us a coffee and chocolate saying, "What it must be like to be stinking rich, living like this all the time?"

I was tired and felt my hair gel rub into the pillowcase. Whoops! Good we were just here for one night. No problem. "Thanks Dad, it's been great!" I muttered as I dozed off. In my head I was telling Mum all about our day, or was it God? Either way, I finished with thanks.

In the morning it was a shame, although we had a massive breakfast, it was too cold to be on the outside of the boat for long. We sat inside the huge pleasure craft with rain pounding on the glass running in streams, "Britain at its best!" Dad moaned. It was good to rest at the back of the boat. I was tired from all that walking yesterday. We got from bridge to bridge across the Smoke really quickly. Athena got a few shots of us in daft poses before we headed back for our bags and the station. I told the girls, "I'm sad to leave London with its thrills but not its crap air, it chokes you!"

"I would like to stay forever!" Athena said.

"Me too! Maybe, in our dreams?" Hannah chirped up. "No, we'll have to do the same when you're here for Uni, if you come."

"Good thinking," said Athena. I think we were ready for the rocking of the train back to the car. Us boys went quiet, only perking up when the trolley with grub came along. Dad had his head in a newspaper. I just scoffed, for a change! I had my earphones in but the girls were well chatty.

"It's gone really well, considering," Dad commented on dropping the girls back at Hannah's. We crashed back at ours to get some quiet before the farewell meal we were gathering for tonight. I would miss Athena but we would always be mates. I hoped Han and I would someday be more. It was a low-key meal, just a Chinese takeaway that Han and her parents, Athena and us shared back here. But it was soon gone. We showed off the pictures taken on our phones to Han's parents. Dad got it out his system how he felt out of the city scene but that it was tolerable for a few days. Athena got beside me and made me promise to keep in touch, no matter what.

I scratched my head saying, "My dad must approve, he's got you watching me through a web cam, now that's scary!"

"No really we should keep friends, John." She gave me one of her looks.

"Okay, I'm listening!" She was there for me when it was the worst. The least I could do is keep her posted when things got better.

We were in my room, when she gave me this church candle saying, "It's for you to light when you feel sad for your mum. I do this for my gran; it works for me - might be worth a try?"

I nodded and hugged her. Too soon it was time for her to go. The last thing she said before going through to 'Departures' was, "Xronia Polla." I looked puzzled so she explained, "Have many more years!"

After scratching my head I said, "Happy New Year and thanks." When she'd gone I told my dad, "You know I once thought Athena would kinda replace Mum." Laughing, as if! Then, Dad and me just chilled till New Year. Not numb like before but all right under the same roof. It had been quite tiring entertaining the girls. Lots of friends rang us to see how we were but we watched the box and ate chocolate, mostly. Oh, and we went to church, to build us up for the New Year. And some more hugs.

Later that week, Dad shared how he wanted to make it better down the youth shelter. He asked if I could help him with a group of my mates, clear it up and paint it. Not a bad idea. I would go with that one. Ben would help; he'd have to - his mum would make him. All part of the bonus of being my oldest friend! But I wasn't the only kid who had to split down there occasionally and Dad knew that.

He cared more and that meant everything. When Dad was settled I thought I'd nip round to Ben's to see what he thought of painting the shelter. It didn't take me long. I'd not seen him since I flung his present his way. It was a joke really. Not a proper present. Mum bought those kind, they took loads of time and effort to shop till you drop for up town. I couldn't be doing with it, so I got him something off ebay, to make him chuckle. It was a survival joke book thing. I thought it was funny. Knocking on his door I got his mum. She was making excuses like not to let me in. I couldn't get me head round it. Anyway I gave her the slip and dived upstairs to his crib. Shocked or what? "What you been up to?" is all I could say. I had so much to tell him but his classic shiner put me off.

He smiled, "What's it to you?" then "Taken up rugby, if you

must know."

"Ace. You need to learn how to run quicker if you want to avoid a battering," is what I told him.

"Like you'd know?" He was a bit down so I changed the subject. "Got any good jokes?" I said, desperate to cheer him up. "And we've got some gigs lined up. Well, they're not entirely gigs but they could be a bit of fun." I laughed hoping he'd join me. "Going on one at the next hols. We're gonna liven up the youth shelter. Put our mark on it legit-wise, with a lick of paint. My dad's sorting the gear out and he'll put on a barbeque for any takers. What do you think?"

"Yeah. Good thinking. It could do with a clean up down there. Dirty pigs, they're slobs some of them who use it. That's the bad news, hard work, what's the good news?" I checked him out; he was having a laugh. He went on, "Go on, tell me what's the other thing?" He was at last showing some interest.

"What's it worth?" I teased him. I ducked expecting a wallop. "Missed," I smiled.

"I owe you a few clouts!" he said.

Random. I went on, "Okay, I'll let you in on the secret. Dad's got this ex-service mate who's just opened up a go-kart track. We're up for some free goes, if you can drag yourself out of bed on Saturday mornings. Apparently no one turns up before eleven so we can warm the karts till the punters show up. How do you fancy having a mess around?"

"Excellent! I'll be there. What time do I need to be up?" He was getting serious about the whole idea.

"Early but if that's a problem you can stop round ours Friday nights. Sorted. It's a bit of a thanks for sticking with us, thing," I said, being real.

"Cheers, sounds good to me. That'll let you off for getting my head kicked in," he surprised me.

I looked at him gone out. Why was he having a fight, anything to do with me? "What's with the black eye?" I asked him. But getting closer I felt him give off these negative waves.

"No problems! Don't worry man, be happy." He sang these words Reggae style.

"See ya then, if ya not talking, man!" I told him realising I'd touched on a sore point.

As usual Han would have to fill me in later. Heading off for home, I texted her. He'd only been sticking up for me! Since I'd left school some yobs at sixth form had been making up rubbish about me, to do with my mum dying. So Ben being Ben he took the lot of them on. No more rumours. They looked much worse than Ben, apparently.

I should text him about him being a mate. But then he already knew that.

13. GETTING IT TOGETHER

January turned out to be like damp slate. Beyond the first couple of grey days when we took the Christmas decorations down and I missed the great company, loomed this newness. Okay, the New Year meant Dad and I were going forward. I did have the go-carting Sat. mornings, as well as youth club now. Quite a party animal! My record was better than Ben's for getting black-flagged, while Dad was definitely the slowest. "Slow and steady wins the race," Dad would say. Not! It was the adrenalin rush that did us well good.

And some more colours came into the frame the day I actually started college. It just couldn't be delayed any more. A real shock! It meant me getting up in the middle of the night, like 6.30 a.m., to catch the stupid-o-clock bus to town. Dad barged in my room all bright and breezy, switched off my alarm saying, "Come on, John, out of that pit." Doing Mum's job. I might as well have woke up with Dad was on his retraining thingy it meant the house was completely empty during the day. It would be handy when he was a qualified driving instructor. Being his first guinea pig I would be bound to pass first time. After all, his reputation depended on it.

Then again, my engineering course was do-able. I missed Ben there but I had to stand on my own two feet, sometime. My tutor was all right, giving me more time to submit stuff because of my grieving situation. Dad had come in and given them a blow-by-blow, of our sob story. It worked! With GCSE retakes coming up, I was working hard at night towards those. So I managed to keep myself out of trouble. But some days were even turning out okay. What was poor was the extreme lack of girls on my course. They were busy, beautician-ing, or something on the next floor. Well, all but Emma. She was the absolute best welder on the whole course and I rated her, mostly; she was neater than me. When she welded her clamp it worked; I just burnt a hole in mine. "Way to go, Emma!" I said.

She'd grinned back, saying, "Stick with me and you might learn something." Cheeky thing! At last I was beginning to get into the swing of a usual day. Almost like I was normal. That night when I got in, I looked at Janet's Christmas card, which was still on my window ledge with details about the weekend in Derbyshire on it. When I was bored in the hols I'd added the date to my awesome Greek `09 calendar, that Athena's dad had sent me. Even though I knew it was marked up there in highlighter, amongst the waves and beach picture. I blanked it making it like a surprise that morning. Granted Dad had been getting lots of washing done. He knew how big this weekend was for me. He'd put Ben off as well. So I had a backpack full of gear for the Saturday morning, when I could have done with a lie in.

Hannah had even texted to say, 'have fun.' Der! I don't know why I wasn't up for it. Maybe I'd become reliant on the boring stuff that was my life! This was another different thing, so my brain had decided not to go there. I was worried that all the stuff about

Mum might be transferred from the safe place I'd stored it filed, **super-mum**. Could I even think about changing it to a shared area? That was a big one. Even worse was having to take on board other kid's sad stories. That could freak me out, I knew. My load of rubbish was enough.

Janet filled me in how some of the kids were there because their gran or granddad had died. So what? Shame. It wasn't their mum, was it? I'd only had one granddad for ages. That was how I felt at first but then Janet said that some grans and granddads were like mums and dads. Her putting me straight helped but I just replied, "It's not normal losing your mum this early, though is it?" This was as we lamely wound our way along the country roads. Sooo boring.

"Of course not!" she sympathised. "Then again, I don't know what is normal. Getting to old age is something some people take for granted, today."

It got me thinking, this growing old issue. Until then I had been happily watching these huge hills. The good thing was I was eying up the gradient for doing an extreme Ollie on my scooter and for a bit of hard ground. That was as my mind was whittled by all the old-age stuff.

Weirdly, staring out of the window I remembered back when Dad had said, "You have permission to shoot me if I ever get as crazy as your granddad, Pete!" But that was before he was my lone parent. That had all changed now. He was no longer allowed to go barking mad. At least that granddad was still alive. I needed to inherit my genes from his side of the family, to stand a chance at a decent length of life. Did my belief change all that, if God had fixed the exact amount of days I was to live? Probably. I could no way pull the plug on this weekend, not with all these questions.

Then I felt sick. Reality check! Thoughts of 'No can do' ran through my mind. No can do this weekend. No can do talking to the other kids. As we pulled up in Janet's lame Nissan Micra I felt I was actually going to throw up. Janet looked at me and then came a daft question, "What's the worst that can happen?" she asked. I don't think even Janet could believe it had come from her mouth either by the way she said, "Oh sorry, sorry John!" Then she ushered me out of the car towards this dull hut. Feeling green. She let me have a minute. That felt better. The handrail could have been a useful grind rail; the one up the ramp to the back door had a good angle on it. I was thinking scootering for a change!

I gave Janet a dirty look. She got that I wasn't impressed. "This is just the meeting place, John and the new sports hall with its climbing wall will be much more you," she told me.

Thank goodness for that! So I was persuaded to go in and with my hood up I crept into this musty hall with lots of random kids, trying not to stand out. "So this is the great weekend that's going to fix everything?" I said. And when a bloke snuck in beside me, I knew he felt the same. He smiled back. I couldn't stop staring at his huge, stained hands.

"How goes it?" he said. "My name's Mike. What you in here for?" He thought he was hilarious and his whole body rocked with laughter. I couldn't help but like him. He could be my new Ben, here.

All I did was nod back. "I'm John, they call me Johnny." Why I said that, I have no idea! Remembering Mum didn't mean sounding like her! What a Wally! I bundled on, "I'm in here down to my mum having cancer and it killing her." But once I got over how big he was I found out that inside he was a lad, like me. Then, he opened up. Mike was 17 he told me and that it was his dad who'd died. Since then, he'd had to run the farm. I gulped. It had taken me all my time to go back to college, never mind doing my mum's jobs. What was his mum doing while Mike did everything? It was different for him. Even harder!

He went on, "The docs told us he'd recover, after he'd had loads of treatment. Don't trust them hospitals, they don't know. My dad was active so they gave him a fighting chance. They gave us these numbers, percentages of him doing okay but after all that they couldn't stop him fading away! Unlucky!" His laughter was gone. I could tell he really loved his dad. He looked well aggravated. He was this giant and there was no chance I wanted to rub him up the wrong way. So I tried to change the subject.

"I'm sorry. It's not fair. You'll be all right here then, with all this macho stuff. Like father like son! You remind me of my dad, he works out a lot. He wonders where he went wrong, with me being more like my mum!"

"Ha!" He nodded saying, "You're right, I've done some stack climbing in my time and loaded a few carts with some bales!"

"And the ladder, have you done that before?" I'd heard about the Jacob's ladder, making out I knew what I was talking about. Dangerous. I should have known better.

"No, but I'll beat you up it!" He was smiling, again. "What actually is this Jacob's ladder thing, then?"

"No idea! My dad goes on about them being good for teamwork. Him being in the Navy, before."

"He sounds a handy sort to have around; I might look him up at harvest time. Can he drive a tractor and trailer?" There was that roar of a born survivor again. Phew! Relief. I couldn't handle him flipping on me.

This blond, wiry woman who'd heard him ask about the ladder, was saying, "Oh, you'll like the Jacob's ladder. Once you've done some wall climbing they give you a go in teams, it's the ultimate challenge. Don't worry about it now though cos it won't be till tomorrow," she was in charge, Amy. And there's me again then worrying about heights. As if I didn't have enough to worry about.

Meanwhile, at least it stopped me thinking about Dad and how he was doing. Another volunteer had told me that the parents would join in the last part of the weekend, when they came to pick us up. That didn't stop me thinking of him, I was worrying about him being alone in the house. It was a good job Sam was going round to take him to the track day booked for him at Christmas. At Donington Park, he would only have the chance to go in a British Touring car! Slamming! And the best thing was Sam was going to get it all on video if he wasn't too quick to catch. So I wasn't missing out, I just hoped he would be okay. Knowing his luck though he'd crash and burn! That's if he hadn't pulled the plug on the idea. He had gone a bit soft lately.

I wondered whether any of the others were scared of their last parent dying or if it was just me being sad. I'd try that question later if I got the chance and give these people here a pop at it because my head couldn't let go of this one.

I'd brought a photo of Mum along with me like I was asked to. Even the helpers had pictures of someone they missed. When we had settled after dropping off our gear in the bedrooms and getting our bearings we all trouped across to this brilliant sports hall. Down at the other side of this wood. Not bad, that. It was well hidden behind these massive trees. It was then that I started to think it might just be all right, this weekend, after all. When we got in there were these great electric blowers warming the place up. I could see some tables laid out with craft stuff on. The girls would enjoy that I thought.

There were more of us than I expected. We soon got into age groups through being grouped by the Mrs. Amy woman. She was okay. "This weekend," she said, "is very confidential. We're sharing important, individual stories which MUST stay here." She pointed. "This is Kevin, an outdoor sports instructor."

At that, Mike nudged me. "Doesn't look as if he could even lift a bale!" Making me smile. Then I realised our badges were colour coded so we could find others in similar situations. Mine was blue so all I needed to do was find other blues. They might get me. We might be able to say, "I know what you're going through," and that'd be cool.

It made me so sad there were so many of us blues. I found it hard to take in the stories of brothers and sisters who'd died. When my mum had her miscarriages she'd shielded me, as ever! Hannah had filled me in on all that. But I never knew so it seemed different. And then I was really young. Whatever, I loved my mum and needed her. That seemed to be the thing that mattered most and could make me angry. I was determined not to cry but some lost it. They made me want to get up and leave. But I was pleased how I held up. I think it was the newbies to this bereavement thing, who caved in. I'd done my crying. Now, fresh out of tears, I understood it was an important part of getting through. The law. It was official. Having a good wail worked!

I made a point of listening to this girl called Claire, when I heard that she'd lost her mum, down to cancer too. I would try to get next her. We might be able to help one another out. Mike was sticking near me whenever he could. Kevin was not too pushy letting us have a go at stuff if we felt like it but Mike told me, "You can do this, no problem!" He was sounding like my dad!

The climbing wall was at the top of this wooded area and quite slippery. Working with the strong ropes helped me take back control and Kevin made it look easy. Dad would never forgive me if I didn't give it everything I'd got. This macho stuff was pushing Mike's buttons too. What all this was doing, cleverly, was getting us to trust one another. And giving us time to concentrate on ourselves in a good way. Like magic we opened up with our tales. The cringe factor completely disappeared at the top of the wall. We were going to scary places, safely.

Some of the girls had real guts. Claire held back at first and was worried about looking stupid but she eventually got up the steep climbing wall and came down slowly. Handling the ropes for one another made us relevant. We could help do something. The climbing was a great leveller. Like fancy dress is at parties. We're welcomed, we make an effort, and then nobody sees the old us. This sharing stuff was dependent on us not only listening but also talking, if we could. Some of us couldn't, they would do more one to one with Kevin later. We learnt to recognise our hurts, as well as strengths.

After a burger and a break to get our breath back, we put on loads of layers under our hoodies and did this blindfolded walk up the hill. We were holding on to a rope but relied on our partner to guide us round. Extra skill was needed for Mike who was a pain to get round. Huge feet went with the hands! When wrong-footed and he landed on your toe it caned. He found it hilarious. I got a bit battered but I took more care with Claire. I think she was used to people letting her down, no way was I being added to her list. This was by moonlight now and I was feeling exhausted, in a good way. The day had been quite intense but not too painful. I'd managed to have a laugh and hold back the tears. Bonus!

As I got in bed Mike had scribbled me his sad history on a scrap of paper. It was all about his dad. I gave him a look to say, sorry. Feeling a bit useless. The bunks were wobbly but they were good enough. He told me that he had to look after his mum. What a great guy. Made me feel like saying, 'ditto' for with my dad but I never. So that night I didn't feel quite so sorry for myself.

On Sunday we made these ace memory boxes. I got glued up making it personal but had fun stuff to put in that reminded me of Mum. Like a jar with different coloured sand in. What was cool was no one knew what the layers of sand meant but me. Like the yellow for her hair or the red left by her lips. And purple for her favourite colour. There was also this useful sticking plaster idea what to do, like when I got angry or fed up. Ways to give myself a break, avoiding explosions. So I told them about our punch bag, hanging in our garage. How it helped. It got a bit of a laugh. Obvious stuff when you thought about it, like going for a run.

Kevin explained, "Don't be tempted to start to use alcohol or drugs to drown your sorrows. They," he told us, "will make things much worse!"

I made little clay models of her favourite things, so I didn't forget. As if? They'd be good to show my kids, apparently, according to the king of the gym, Kevin. It was quite calming. That and some candle lighting with chillaxing sounds. Whilst we were making he asked, "Does anyone want to hear about my story? The story of my brother's death?"

I did, so I listened to the bit about them playing as kids by the river. Like wallies! Can't tell, not going there cos it's private. He told us how he'd bottled up all these bad feelings, with no one there to talk to but his family for years. And that just made it all the more difficult to get over. He blamed himself when it was really an accident. Kids could be cruel about these things and some ignorant adults, who ought to know better. He assured us there was lots of help for those grieving now. He gave us a list of websites. So he knew what he was talking about. Poor him. I saw Mike was getting a bit tired with all the hype. He was stressing, needed air, so he headed back with his box full of about his dad.

I helped clear up saying, "It's been good cos I haven't had to hold any feelings back and it's helped." That's what I told Kevin who was made up for me that I could be real. I even went for it mentioning my worries about my dad ever dying. He let me know that it wasn't unusual to feel insecure and worry about health after losing your parent to something like cancer.

"Just get through one day at a time," he said and then. "The thing is, not to panic! Keep talking. You don't have to do this alone. Your dad was in the Navy wasn't he? They keep them pretty fit in the forces with all that training. Good docs too. And he's not on his own either. Just think about all the friends and family who will help your dad." Straight away I thought of Sam and Paul. I told him about Janet and even Joan and the fussy cake makers too. I told him how tough Dad had found his life changing and how we'd spent Mum's insurance money sailing away to avoid the pain. He reminded me about getting proper mates around us. He reassured me and said to ring the Bereavement Centre again, if there was ever I wanted to talk more to Amy.

So when Dad arrived I'd pulled myself together having just been through my paces up the ladder and down. I was in a right sweat. They'd conned us into small groups, with these crafts activities letting down any last barriers and let us believe we could actually tackle this monster. Amy was even taking photos of us in a tangled mass, swinging over ropes on harnesses. Not a pretty sight! But funny, when it was my turn to watch. We spent a lot of time shouting at each other to put their backs into the job. That mostly worked. We were supposed to just help our team but we all just mucked in. Mike the anchor was having the rope go nowhere! But when he was going up the ladder himself he was a bit heavy and got a wobble on. Earthquakes came to mind! My stomach was doing somersaults. I shouted at him, "Steady Mike!" Thinking if he didn't stop rocking it they'd all end up on the ground in a heap. He had more bulk to heave up than us!

When he stopped being a clown he did the job of pulling up the team to the top bar easily having mastered the whole balance thing. He gave these masterful instructions that were a bit dodgy. So it was up to me to help him out. Teamwork at its best! What was awesome, for once me being skinny helped. I got up without looking a complete plonker. Bonus! Me being last up I'd shoved the last stragglers up to him and there we clung victorious. Sorted! Top team. We made an awful racket; relief probably.

I had tried to tell Dad all this, when he arrived he asked, "What've you been up to?"

Instead I said, "Not much!" With me looking hot and sweaty

he raised his eyebrows unconvinced until I asked him, "And how was your touring car drive, any more war wounds?"

Then he gave me the wait till I get you home look saying, "I was super-quick, as expected and no, thank-you, I stuck to the track like glue. Well, I got away with it, nice circuit! Sam said I looked quite professional!"

"No skid marks, then?" I was laughing at teasing him but he got me and squeezed me into a, "Didn't mean it!" Calming down we picked up on the whole point of the weekend, like dealing with our issues. And I noticed he was being great.

"How's it gone?" He asked me again, interested.

"Sorted! It's been brilliant. I've learnt about those happy things in my brain and how to bring them on. Endorphins or something? Doing exercise is actually good for me, they say." I laughed watching my dad give me a 'gone out' look. "We've built up trust and done some crazy stuff like scream and shout about our parents dying. Then, we thought how we felt about it all. We found out about good grief. There's even a website about finding different ways of dealing with loss. It's got some awesome games on. For the scary bits, they made us write our shitty feelings down on some paper and then we threw clay bombs at it! With some force, I tell you. Pretty awesome! Basically, I think this 'getting over it' takes time. They tell me it's a process we're going through that's different for us all."

Dad nodded. "It sounds as though you've got a lot out of it, I'm pleased. You know, sometimes I don't know what to say to you..." He started to apologise for not knowing how to mourn. Or was it for being crap at it? Anyway, it didn't matter.

I thought best to stop him with, "Oh and I've just had a go at one of those Jacob's Ladders you've done in training. Easy! My mate Mike made that one, ace!" I dragged my dad over from the car park to see the mighty pile of wood I'd climbed up. "And there's photos to prove it, if you don't believe me," I said, shoving my phone with the evidence under his nose.

"Not bad, no, I do. I believe you. Quite an effort!" He smiled, for once not wanting to outdo me. I'm sure he'd done far bigger and better efforts in his time. But he left it and told me, "Today, I've been to talk to your mother at the grave. I've been doing that a lot lately. Paul has shown me how to pray to Jesus just like I talk to your mum. He says I'll get a reply from God. And that praying will help me trust Jesus with her."

"Does he?" I nodded remembering Paul telling me something similar, not long ago. "It helps me, Dad, praying. I did quite a lot on the climbing wall!"

I made a joke, filling him in that it was okay. I wanted him to know we'd be okay and that we'd got the best help. He nodded and smiled. I was remembering when the cramp went and at last I could breathe again. When I started to let God have it all in my prayers and panic was over.

There was this prize-giving thing in the hall, right at the end. It was neat when Mike gave me a certificate for helping him on the climbing wall. Or was it the other way round? A big deal, that meant something! Mine was for Claire, who got more than half way up Jacob's ladder, despite being absolutely petrified. Dad gave me an approving nudge, after I gave her that. Us three, Mike, Claire and me, would keep in touch. There was already some talk of reunions and we hadn't gone yet. When I met Mike's mum I wanted to hug her but I couldn't. She was lovely. We let balloons go at the end. Sending 'God bless' messages up to heaven for Annie. A bit emotional, really. After taking every ones emails and saying thanks we chucked my stuff in the car and said our goodbyes. I must have fallen asleep within minutes of getting in the car; I can't remember the drive back.

I dragged myself in from the car. Then I snacked a bit and had a quick shower. Whilst I flipped through these lovely messages on my mobile I needed to get back to, from great gals like Hannah, I couldn't be asked. Later. One day at a time. I shouted down, "Night Dad, it's good to be home."

He popped his head in, having rushed upstairs, "Missed you too, son," is all he said.

14. MOVING FORWARDS

The next day was a busy Monday. It was getting easier despite being dog-tired. Dad and I were talking. So after college, while my dad was about, I made the best of it telling him how much better I felt recently. "Dad, when I was praying with Paul, Friday night after youth club, I felt this arm around me. It was far out! I had to do a double take but it was there, for sure. And at first I thought it was Mum sending me these positive waves but Paul said that it's Jesus. It's Jesus who wants to comfort me." I was watching his face to make sure I didn't freak him out. But he was taking it in. I held back the tears that came from him actually listening to me.

"That's like what your mum told me. She said she was safe with God holding her hand. That's why she wasn't scared to die. And that the whole of the kingdom of heaven was open to her, so she would be fine!" He sighed. "I'm beginning to understand, sorry, for me it takes time to sink in."

"Dad, I think I've learnt more since Mum's death because I've asked more questions. Real important questions, that meant everything. Whilst I knew some of the answers, they were still hard to take. And when I don't like them it's my problem. Somehow, to get answers I have to chill and wait." He nodded and smiled back at me.

"Good tip, son! I should have listened years ago, when your mum tried to let me in on her good news. I missed out then but I'm not going to with you, John. I want to know where you're coming from. You know that, don't you?"

I believed him. So I nodded. He had a huge chance. We both needed to make the most of that. So we tried to get back into our routine. Normal life, whatever that was? That was after I'd watched this flash video of my dad, tearing around the track at Donington like a mad man! It was brilliant. Sam was screaming as he videoed which was even funnier. Now we both had a few more friends who knew exactly where we were coming from. Bargain! And Dad and I were putting up with each other.

What I was just gob-smacked to hear about was, after Mum's memorial service planned for the summer, we were also going to have a baptism. Of all things, random! And I was thinking of a baby, wrong! It was only going to be my dad's baptism. After all those holy huddles with Paul, when he said he was finding healing, he'd gone and found Jesus. I hoped it would help him forget about Iraq and all his scary rubbish that used to give him nightmares. He really needed to stop worrying about all that. Go forward and give himself a break.

It got me thinking about who our mates were, lately. Mum's friends from church had kind of adopted us, sticking to us through the worst times. I used to think that they were different down there, tight with one another but we were different now too, so that was okay. Other old friends, who liked Mum and Dad as an item, backed off us when Dad was a one-parent family. Dad said, "We don't need fair-weather friends; we're better off without them." Some so-called friends, who came to the funeral, crossed the road when they saw us, since when they didn't know what to say. Pathetic! Then again, Dad had backed off his mates like Jack next-door when all his answers came from a beer bottle and Dad had tried that with whisky; it didn't work.

Now, Dad dropped in to help out places, doing stuff for free, if he hadn't got any driving lessons booked. He went on the youth club rota to make chips and do lifts, when I let him. I needed my space too and he knew that. I tried to stay cool avoiding dodgy sorts to stay out of trouble. Those numb days, when I couldn't give a damn were over for me. My old life had changed. We were a bit square now. When Dad wasn't teaching one of my mates driving he'd take me out and teach me in his flashy, silver, duel control Fiesta. Check him out! He was giving decent discounts to my mates so quite a few had signed up to a block of ten lessons. I had to be the first to pass of us lot, but with my theory test under my belt in six months time, I reckoned it was doable. There was this rich kid who would probably beat me. He didn't count. Not bothered.

There was a new idea for spending Mum's booklet money. The fund was accumulating steadily; as more hospices found out about it they requested a few copies. I met someone last week that gave me a brill idea. Thursday last week we were winding down fish and chips from the Chippie van, when the doorbell rang. With the nights getting lighter it must have been just past six because it was hard to see who stood at our front door. Till I put the outside light on. There stood Emily, this girl who'd disappeared from my maths class, at the end of year 12. For no reason, only I thought she'd bottled it on her exams. Fair enough. She'd gone to live in town. Han had mentioned it to me over Christmas. And behind her was only a buggy with a kid in! I was completely gob-smacked! It was a foul, rainy night, so of course she came in.

"Do you remember me John, from school? It's Emily," she said. "And this young man's called Sonny," while pointing to the hooded tiny person. "Sorry, I had to come… you see, I met your mum just before she died. And she was so kind to me. I wanted you to know." The words came out rehearsed and her shoulders relaxed as she finished, like it had been difficult to say. She used to be quiet at school. Ha!

Interested to know more, I took her coat and helped her get the buggy into our kitchen, where the muddy wheels wouldn't matter. It meant picking my college stuff up from the bottom of the stairs. Carefully hanging her coat on the banister I shoved my bag one step nearer my room. I pictured Athena's 'tut-tut!' look. The one she'd gone and passed on to Hannah to keep me in line. When I wasn't a good lad. Worse luck.

Dad said, "Hello Sonny," to the baby first, overhearing our conversation. The fact that the baby was asleep didn't faze him, as if we always had kids round our house. "My name's Steve; I'm John's dad. Thanks for coming and if you were a friend of Annie's then you're a friend of mine. Do you want a hot drink or can I get the baby anything?"

"No, I can't stay long; I'm on the number 22 bus back to

Melton. He's fine, ta. But can I have some kitchen roll, please, to wipe the buggy hood?" she said, sitting down at our kitchen table. Dad just did as asked, being all right. But not moving.

As she got on with fussing over the sleeping baby, wiping the rain off the hood, I had to ask, "Where did you meet my mum then?"

"It was up the hospital, when I first found out I was pregnant." As she said it her cheeks went red. "She told me that she recognised me from seeing us at school and she knew my mum. Let me just say, I was crying about a big change coming up in my life, having him," she rocked the buggy, "at the same time as she was worrying about leaving you two."

Dad had to sit down joining us at the table, hearing that. Gob-smacked. The colour drained from his face, he looked a bit sad.

Picking up on this she added, "She was angry that she was dying but had the time to think of me. Amazing! I was thinking wicked thoughts about Sonny and she made it easier to see him as a good thing. She must have talked for half an hour about how wonderful it was when you were born, John. And that you were the absolute best!"

Now, she got me gulping! "Of course," I boasted, feeling myself go well hot.

"But I've just come to say how much of a difference she made in my life. Without me asking, she offered me this money to go shopping for new baby things. After that I never looked back.

She told me how writing this booklet thing helped her manage her sadness at leaving you two, who she loved so much. And she taught me that family is everything. What life's all about."

Dad pulled himself together saying, "Well we're glad it's working out for you, Emily. I know she would have been delighted about your Sonny. You're right, she loved life, and babies especially. Thanks so much for bringing him to see us and please keep in touch."

She just sat there glad to have got it all out. Dad broke the silence. "Now, are you sure I can't take you back to town in the car, it really isn't any bother? It'll give John some experience of driving in the dark, on the way back, albeit on the old airfield."

So she eventually let us drive them back home. She promised to keep us updated on Sonny's progress. Dad asked if he could wave if he saw them in town. A bit much, that! But amazingly, she agreed. And I did get a go driving on the way back. It was a quiet journey as we were both shell-shocked to hear Mum had struggled with leaving us. Deep down we knew. We thought it had been easier for her, with believing she was going to a better place. This somehow proved to us that she loved us. "You know Dad? When I see Sonny I can think, well, that people have to die to make room for little babies like him." Dad was watching my driving, checking there was no one behind us. "We wouldn't have been this close either. Not until you retired." Still I couldn't get a reaction from him. That's when I had my great idea, so I told Dad, "We'll go for giving a gift to help a local kid who's struggling. That's what we'll do with Mum's money. There won't be anything to look at but it will make a real difference in a mate's life. Reaching out, when they've got it rough." I sat back pleased with my effort. Then had a revelation, "You know who'd help us with that don't you?"

"I'm one step ahead of you. You mean Paul don't you? Paul's a natural at picking up on the sad and lonely. Well, he helped me didn't he?" Dad nudged me, grinning. "We could let him give it out too, so as not to embarrass anyone," he said, nodding manically. By the time we got home it was agreed. A low-key affair, a donation to someone down on his luck, no strings attached! Could even be someone with a bad habit who needed specialist support, hmm. Let's see. That got me thinking. There were a few I could think of. It would be great if Joe were ready to take help. Who knows what nightmare he was going through and we didn't want to read about him, after an O.D. Yeah, Mum would love that. Helping those who others didn't bother with, down to them being hard to help mostly. I told him, "Think of Joe, as my long lost brother." Dad gave me this long look. He wasn't going there, fair enough!

We'd do it, give out the donation just before Mum's memorial. What a great way to remember her goodness and for it to live on. It would be fun, too. Dad got cracking working towards the big day, meeting up with Paul's small group from church who came round once a week, to help him. He was letting everyone who cared about Mum, have an invite, 'Annie's Memorial Service and Steve's Baptism,' it said. He even gave me a handful to give to my mates. Ben would be there for sure. My dad came out with it saying, "It seems the right time. I want everyone who loved our Annie to know that I'm safe. They might stop worrying about me, then! It's just a pity your mum can't be there." I knew this was what she had prayed for.

I remembered when Mum had her baptism that it was after a lot of bible reading to put her mind at rest about all the big stuff, like dying. She was calmer after that, a bit surreal. This is when she talked about her new life. I never dreamt Dad would follow so soon, his beliefs changed with his circumstances.

And then, der! Reality-check time, so I went and asked, "But you're not planning leaving me soon, are you Dad?" Like a complete idiot! I knew he was fine but had to check.

He went to me, "What are you like? I'm fit as a butcher's dog, me, I just want it all sewn up, that's all. Call it playing it safe, if you want. Then again, ask me how my heart is after I've taking you for your driving test!"

"Ha, ha! You're so funny! Not!" But what he was saying was he would be there for me. I needed to know that. Going on I said, "In Mum's letter, it said that there's a house with many rooms in heaven, enough for us all. Did you get that bit, too? That's why some old people were saying Mum's been called home, at the funeral. I get it now. Can you just imagine her fluffing up our pillows till it's our time to join her?"

Dad gave it a minute, then replied, "Yes, I can. But that's too far off to even think about yet and you've got some work to do, young man."

Dobbing my head I gave him a, "Yes boss!" Then moved out of his reach, smiling.

"Me boss? You're having a laugh! I used to think I was, in the Navy. Totally unaware of God then, I was. No, I'm just being held like that little baby Sonny is held by his mum, Emily." And it's a great feeling. Your mum moved over to give me more time with you. You're spot on, John."

It was then that I began to realise we were going to be all right. Now I'd got my dad in a safe place. We were solid.

I even took after him, they say!

We could do this, together. Right.

R.I.P. Annie Jane White- Miss you loads forget you never.

Matthew 5:4:
"Blessed are those who mourn, for they will be comforted."

Useful Websites

Childhood Bereavement Network	www.childhoodbereavementnetwork.org.uk
Winston's Wish	www.winstonswish.org.uk
Care for the Family	www.careforthefamily.org.uk
Facing Bereavement	www.facingbereavement.co.uk
Youth In Mind	www.youthinmind.co.uk
The Road For You	www.rd4u.org.uk
Child Bereavement	www.childbereavement.org.uk
Mind Organisation for better Mental Health	www.mind.org.uk/
The BBC	www.bbc.co.uk/relationships
Family Caring Trust	www.familycaring@co.uk
Childline	www.childline.org.uk
Riprap-When a parent dies	www.riprap.org.uk
The Way Foundation for bereaved and children	www.wayfoundation.org.uk
National Council for one parent families	www.oneparentfamilies.org.uk
Cruse Bereavement Care	www.crusebereavementcare.org.uk
Marie Curie Foundation	www.mariecurie.org.uk
Barnardo's	www.barnardos.org.uk